GREEK'S BABY
OF REDEMPTION

GREEK'S BABY OF REDEMPTION

KATE HEWITT

MILLS & BOON

First published in Great Britain 2019
by Mills & Boon, an imprint of HarperCollins*Publishers*
1 London Bridge Street, London, SE1 9GF

Large Print edition 2019

© 2019 Kate Hewitt

ISBN: 978-0-263-08282-1

MIX
Paper from
responsible sources
FSC C007454

This book is produced from independently certified
FSC™ paper to ensure responsible forest management. For
more information visit www.harpercollins.co.uk/green.

FALKIRK COUNCIL LIBRARIES

Printed and bound in Great Britain
by CPI Group (UK) Ltd, Croydon, CR0 4YY

CHAPTER ONE

'STAY.'

Milly James stilled, shock racing through her at the sound of that single word, uttered in a husky voice by a man she'd never actually seen in person. Her employer.

'Pardon...?' She turned around slowly, blinking into the dim gloom of the wood-panelled study, the curtains drawn against the Aegean's azure sky, the tiniest sliver of lemony sunlight peeking through the heavy material. It was a beautiful summer's day, but in the gloomy shroud of the study it could have been the depths of a dark winter's night, the thick stone walls of the villa keeping out the island's baking heat.

'Stay.'

It was clearly a command, uttered with brusque authority, and so slowly she closed the door, the final-sounding click echoing in through the room.

She hadn't even realised he was in the study when she'd opened the door to do her usual dusting, only to stumble back at the sight of him sitting in the shadows, barely visible.

Alexandro Santos' instructions had been clear—he was not to be disturbed. Ever. And now she'd unwittingly done just that, because she'd heard the car motor starting and she'd thought he'd gone out. Her heart climbed its way to her throat as she tried to make him out through the gloom. Was he angry? How could she have been so careless? 'I'm sorry, Kyrie Santos. I didn't realise you were here. Is…is there something you need?' she asked in as steady a voice as she could.

In the nearly six months since she'd been hired as housekeeper by Alexandro Santos, she'd never spoken to him, save for the first, rather abrupt conversation on the telephone when he'd offered her employment. This was the first time he'd been back to his luxurious retreat on the Greek island of Naxos since she'd started work, and she'd been tiptoeing around the villa for the last two days, trying to avoid him since he'd made it so clear he didn't want to be bothered. At *all*. And now she might have messed it up completely.

'I'm very sorry,' she blurted, wishing he would say something to break the taut silence. 'I won't disturb you again...'

'Never mind that.' He dismissed her words with a flick of his fingers; she sensed the movement rather than saw it. 'You asked if I needed something, Miss James.' He spoke in a cold drawl, more than a hint of darkness in his tone. She wished she could see his face; the room was so very dark, and the sliver of light barely touched the top of his midnight-dark head.

She blinked, her eyes straining to see more, and, as if he sensed her scrutiny, he moved from where he'd been sitting behind his desk, walking to the window so his back was to her, the light gilding his outline in gold—all six feet three of powerfully built man, his crisp white shirt stretching tautly across his back and broad shoulders.

'Yes,' he answered his own question. 'I do need something.'

'Then how can I help you?' Milly asked, glad that there might be something she could do. 'Would you like a meal…or the room tidied…?' She trailed off, because she had the sudden, inexplicable sense that he didn't want either of those things, and she felt foolish for offering them.

Alexandro Santos didn't answer her. He hadn't moved, and she still couldn't see his face. She knew what he looked like from the Internet search she'd done when she'd first been hired: dark hair, sculpted cheekbones, cold, blue eyes, a body of leashed and lethal power.

Ridiculously handsome, but in a way that had trailed a chilly finger of unease along her spine. He'd looked both intent and remote, a fierce determination in those blue, blue eyes, a sense of distance about him so even in a crowd he stood out, apart. Now she couldn't see him at all, and that wasn't any better.

'How long have you been working for me, Miss James?' he asked after another endless moment.

'Nearly six months.' Milly shifted where she stood, trying not to fidget. He had no reason to fire her, surely? No cause for complaint. For the last five and a half months she'd kept the villa clean, helped in the garden, and paid all the household bills. As housekeeper for a house that was empty most of the time, she knew she had an easy job, but she loved the villa and the island of Naxos, and she'd been very glad for the work—and the pay.

Although some might have found her life lonely, it suited Milly perfectly. After too many years on the fringes of her parents' chaotic social scene, bounced from boarding school to boarding school, with an endless round of vapid and dissipated parties in between, she'd been looking forward to some solitude…as well as the extremely generous salary Alexandro had offered. He couldn't take it away now, not when she was getting closer to saving the kind of money she needed to make Anna safe and happy, for ever.

'Six months.' Alexandro turned slightly so she could make out his profile—the close-cut dark hair, the straight nose, the angled cheekbone and full lip. He looked like a statue—a dark, dangerous and beautiful block of marble, perfect and so very cold. Even in the dim room, she sensed a remoteness about him, a certain distance in the way he held his body, angled his head. 'Are you happy here?'

'Happy?' The question, the *idea*, startled her. Why should he care for her happiness? 'Yes. Very.'

'It must be rather lonely, though.'

'I don't mind my own company.' She relaxed a fraction, because it seemed as if he were merely concerned for her welfare. And yet... that didn't seem like her employer at all, a man who, according to the Internet, at least, was a cold, driven workaholic, with whispers of ruthlessness towards his competitors. A man who was photographed at various social scenes looking hard and unsmiling; sometimes there would be an elegant woman draped on his arm, but he rarely paid them any attention, at least in the photos and videos she'd looked at. It was almost as if they weren't there at all.

'Still, you're quite young.' He paused, and Milly waited. 'How old...?'

'Twenty-four.' Which he must have known from her rather brief and unremarkable CV.

'And you went to university...'

'Yes, in England.' Four years studying modern languages, and she was fluent in Italian and French as well as her native English, and now she had a smattering of Greek, as well. But Alexandro Santos knew all this.

'Surely you have more ambition, then?' he asked. 'Than cleaning rooms…?'

'I'm perfectly happy as I am, Kyrie Santos.'

'Please, call me Alex.' She remained silent. 'You haven't considered moving back to Paris? You were working as a translator, I believe, before you came here?'

'Yes.' And being paid peanuts compared to her salary now. She thought of her days in a drab office, translating dreary business letters. Then she thought of Philippe, with his golden hair and gleaming smile, his oh-so-honeyed words, and her insides shuddered. 'I have no desire to go back to Paris, Kyrie—'

'Alex.'

She said nothing, uncertain and again on edge, wondering where this unsettling line of inquiry was meant to lead.

'What about romance?' he asked abruptly, shocking her. 'A husband, children…? Do you want those things, eventually?'

Milly hesitated, unsure how to respond. Surely the question was inappropriate, com-

ing from an employer? And yet how could she
not answer?

'I ask because I prefer continuity,' Alex resumed, almost as if he'd been able to read her
thoughts. 'If you're going to leave after a year
to follow some man...'

'I am not going to *follow some man*,' Milly
retorted with stiff dignity. Once upon a time,
she would have followed Philippe. She would
have followed him anywhere, until she'd found
out the truth. Until he'd told her. Even now she
could recall the mocking glint in his eyes, the
cruel twist to his mouth. She forced the image
away and focused on Alex Santos, even though
she could barely see him. 'The question is offensive.'

'Is it?' Alex continued to gaze out through
the crack between the curtains. It was impossible to tell what he was thinking. She felt like
a prop in a play, something he could almost
forget was there. And yet he was asking her
such personal questions...*why*? 'And what of
children?' he asked after another long moment.

Milly tried not to gape. 'I haven't thought
about that,' she said at last. 'I'm not interested
in having children now, at any rate.'

'Not now? Or not ever?'

Milly shrugged helplessly. 'Certainly not now. And perhaps not ever. Not any time soon.' She knew how fractured and fraught families could be, and while on some level she might have the maternal instinct most women possessed, she had no desire to kick-start it. Anna was her primary concern.

'So you do not wish to have children?'

Milly felt herself flush. Why was he trying to pin her down on this? 'Maybe one day,' she half muttered. 'I haven't thought that far ahead. But really, I can't see how it is any concern of yours.'

'Perhaps you will.'

'I'm sorry…?' He didn't answer and she released the pent-up breath that had bottled inside her lungs. 'Is that all, Kyrie… Alex?' she finally asked. 'If so, I'll go now…'

'That's not all.' His words stopped her in her tracks. 'I have a proposition for you, Miss James.'

'A proposition?' She didn't like the sound of *that*. The word was loaded with meaning, laced with innuendo, even when spoken in Alexandro Santos' curt tone. 'I'm not sure I…'

'A perfectly respectable one. As respectable as one could possibly be, in fact.' A note of rather bleak humour that she didn't understand had entered his voice, and so she simply waited, having no idea how to respond. 'A business offer,' Alex clarified. 'A very generous one. You accepted this position because of the salary, did you not?'

'Yes...' And to get away from Paris and the mocking eyes of Philippe and his crowd, but she wasn't about to go into that.

'Money is an incentive to you?'

'Financial stability is.' And saving money for Anna, but that was something else she had no intention of explaining. It was all too complicated, too sad and too sordid, and her employer did not need to know her personal details.

'And my business proposition will certainly give you financial stability. In fact, that might be considered its chief benefit. But I admit, it might seem, at first glance, a rather unconventional idea.' He let out a humourless rasp of laughter that would have chilled her if it hadn't seemed so despairing. 'Although perhaps not, considering how sensible and level-headed you seem. I think you might well see the practical advantages.'

'Thank you, I think?' Milly gazed at him uneasily, completely out of her depth. 'But I really have no idea what you're talking about. What is this...business proposition?'

Although she wasn't sure she really wanted to know. Whatever it was, it didn't sound like something expected or normal. What could he possibly want from her, in exchange for *money*?

She wasn't naïve; neither was she, sadly, that innocent. She had an inkling of what he might want, and yet she could hardly credit such a possibility. She knew she wasn't pretty— mousy-brown hair, same coloured eyes, a slight, unassuming figure. She wasn't the sort to incite impassioned desire in any man, never mind what she'd once foolishly, so foolishly, let herself believe, with stars in her eyes and fairy tales in her heart. But she wasn't going to think about Philippe.

And it would be just as foolish now to imagine that a man like Alexandro Santos, a handsome billionaire who could probably have any woman he wanted, was interested in her in that way. It was laughable, utterly so, and she would do well to remember that. Just looking at him now, shrouded in darkness, emanating a dark and innate authority as well as an undeniable charisma, made her realise how far apart they were in their experiences. Even when she couldn't see him, she *felt* him, like an electric pulse in the air—dangerous and exciting, and definitely off-limits.

Yet what *could* he want? What else did she *have*? Her mind darted into possible corners, disliking what she imagined there. What if he was into something...well, *strange*? Some kind of fetish or weird kink he wouldn't dare suggest to anyone he considered respectable...but no, she was being really fanciful now. Maybe he simply wanted her housekeeping services.

Perhaps he wanted to fly her to Athens to clean his penthouse there. But Milly knew she was fooling herself. Dusting and sweeping were hardly the most marketable or desirable skills, and it was obvious whatever Alex Santos was about to suggest was something out of the ordinary.

'Kyrie Santos...'

'Alex.'

'Alex.' She made herself repeat his name, the syllables sounding sharp as they came out of her mouth, like the pins turning in a lock. He still hadn't turned, hadn't spoken. 'Are you going to tell me what this proposition of yours is?'

He didn't turn from the window as he answered, his voice flat, toneless, without any warmth. 'I want you to marry me.'

Although Alex remained staring out of the window so Milly couldn't see his full face, he felt her shock. It rippled through the room like an electric current, pulsing between them with a dangerous charge. He angled his head so he could glance back at her, his eyes straining in the darkness. Her own almond-brown eyes widened, her pink lips parting.

She wasn't a beautiful woman by any means, but there was something compelling about her slender frame, the innate dignity in the proud set of her shoulders, the tilt of her chin. To his surprise, Alex felt a shaft of interest slice through him—desire, something he hadn't felt in years. That was rather inconvenient.

'You're...you're not serious,' she finally stammered.

'I assure you, I am.'

'Why would you want to marry *me*?'

It was, of course, an excellent question, and one Alex intended to answer truthfully. There would be no games in their marriage, no pretence in what he intended to be an extremely straightforward transaction. 'Because I don't have the time to find a more suitable and willing woman—'

'Wow, thanks.' The words burst out of her, full of hurt bitterness.

'And,' he continued implacably, 'I need an heir as soon as possible.'

Milly reeled back, hitting the door, her hand fumbling for the knob. 'Don't be alarmed,' Alex said. 'I'm trying to be truthful. It would be foolish for either of us to pretend, even for a moment, that a marriage between us would be anything more than a business arrangement, one involving courtesy and respect on both sides, of course.'

'And yet you said an *heir*...'

'This would not be a marriage in name only, obviously.' He still spoke calmly, but images danced through his mind all the same. Skin burnished gold by candlelight, light brown hair loose on bare, freckled shoulders. Absurd, because their marriage would never be like *that*, and he didn't even know if she had freckles.

'Obviously...' Milly repeated faintly, still looking stunned.

'And time is rather of the essence, although we can discuss the particulars—assuming you are agreeable.'

'Agreeable—' The word came out in a squeak. He'd shocked her, clearly, and she hadn't even seen his face yet. The thought almost made Alex laugh, except he hadn't actually found anything funny in months. Twenty-two months, to be precise. 'Kyrie Santos,' she said firmly, once she'd recovered her composure. 'I am *not* agreeable.'

'You haven't even heard the terms.'

'I don't need to hear the terms. I'm not in the habit of selling myself.'

'We'd be married,' Alex pointed out reasonably. 'It would hardly be classified as that.'

'It would be to me.' She shook her head, a shudder running through her whole body, a visceral reaction of something close to disgust, which caught him on the raw. She hadn't even *seen* him yet. 'I'm sorry, but no. Never.' She spoke with such vehemence that he was intrigued as well as irritated. It was exceedingly inconvenient for her to refuse.

'You almost sound as if you've had such an offer before,' he remarked. 'The way you're reacting, as if you're remembering something offensive. As if my proposition recalls another.'

'Of course it doesn't!'

'Of course?' he queried, arching an eyebrow, the one she could see.

'Most men are not in the habit of making such propositions,' Milly said in that same chilly voice of maidenly affront. She donned that voice like a dress—something that could be taken off as needed, a bit of flimsy armour. It made him wonder what she was protecting underneath.

'Aren't they?' he queried. 'Most marriages are business deals of some kind, Miss James. A negotiation of sorts, no matter what emotional underpinnings they possess.'

'And yet our marriage would have no *emotional underpinning*,' she returned. 'I don't even know you. I've never met you before today.'

'That is not out of the ordinary, for situations such as this.'

'What makes you think I want to get married?'

'Nothing. Like I said, this would be a business arrangement. And the financial stability is what I think you will find attractive about this proposition.' He let out a huff of laughter. 'Nothing else.'

She stayed silent, and Alex turned slightly, wanting to see her face, able to make it out in the dim room only a little. Her eyes were wide, her lips pressed together.

She looked uneasy, but she also looked… torn. Her hand had slipped from the doorknob, and now her fingers were knotted together. As he gazed at her, she nibbled her lip, her eyes darting this way and that. She looked, he realised, as if part of her was tempted or at least intrigued by his offer, but she didn't want to admit it.

'Financial stability,' she finally said. 'What do you mean by that?'

'I would make marriage worth your while.'

He waited, to see if she asked more, but she shook her head.

'Now *that* sounds like selling myself, and to a stranger. I think any marriage should have some kind of emotional foundation, if not love.'

He cocked his head. 'You almost sound cynical.'

'Cynical—?'

'As if you don't really believe what you're saying,' he clarified. 'You want to, but you don't.'

'What I believe or don't believe is of no concern to you, and of no relevance to this conversation,' she returned sharply. 'The answer is still no.'

'Why?' Alex asked, letting his voice loosen into a lazy drawl. 'Out of interest?'

'Why?' She looked and sounded incredulous, but also up against a wall. Figuratively as well as literally, her back pressed to the door, her chest heaving so he could see the rise and fall of her small breasts. A few wisps of light brown hair had escaped from her normally neat ponytail, framing her heart-shaped face. She was, he decided with some surprise, quite lovely. When he'd made the decision to

marry her, her looks had not been part of the equation. She was convenient, suitable, and her lowly position meant he would be able to manage her. That was all he required.

'Yes, why?' he reiterated. 'Why are you not willing even to consider my offer? Not even a single question as to the nature of our arrangement?'

'You've already made the *nature* quite clear—'

'You mean sex?'

'Well, yes,' she nearly spluttered.

'You object to having sex with your husband?'

'I object to marrying someone I don't feel anything for, someone I don't even *know*—'

'Yet people have been doing that for centuries. Millennia.'

'Even so…'

'You told me you weren't interested in romance.'

'Not at this point in my life, no.'

'Or perhaps ever, I believe your words were. So…?'

'That doesn't mean I want to marry *you*.'

She sounded exasperated now. Alex allowed himself a cold little smile.

'Would five million euros change your thinking?'

Her mouth opened. Closed. And then again. Her eyes wide and as brown and soft as pansies. 'That's a lot of money,' she finally said, her voice faint.

'Indeed.' He cocked his head. 'Would you like to hear the particulars now?'

She bit her lip. 'You think I'll change my mind simply because of money? That's insulting.'

'Financial stability,' he reminded her. 'It's a powerful incentive.'

'I'm not some gold-digger.' The words burst out of her, like an old wound breaking open. Alex wondered at it.

'I know you're not.'

'I won't sell myself.'

'So you keep saying, but to think of it that way is distasteful. We are talking marriage, remember. Not being a mistress.'

'Yet it's true nevertheless.'

'Not necessarily. It's a deal, Miss James. We both get something out of it.'

She shook her head slowly, her eyes still wide. 'Considering the nature of our conversation, perhaps you should call me Milly.'

Victory loomed closer, elusive but possible. Probable, even. She hadn't stormed out of the room. She hadn't slapped his face. She hadn't seen it, either. They would get to that all in good time. 'Very well, Milly. Why don't you take a seat?'

'All right.' Milly walked with careful, deliberate steps to one of the leather club chairs in front of his desk and sank into it, ankles neatly crossed, hands linked at her waist like a respectable matron. 'Can we turn the light on?' she asked. 'I can barely make you out, and I've never actually seen you in person, which seems ridiculous considering the nature of our discussion.'

He tensed, and then made himself relax. 'I'm averse to light.'

'You're not a vampire, are you?' It was obviously a joke, but she still sounded uncertain.

'No, most certainly not.' He turned to face her, angling his head in a way he knew would hide the worst. 'I'll turn it on in a moment, perhaps, after we've discussed some of the details.'

'Why me?' Milly asked bluntly. 'Why not someone far more suitable?'

'Because you're here,' Alex answered just as bluntly. 'And you're happy to remain on this island. And in the six months you've been in my employ, you've seemed trustworthy and hardworking, or so my man here, Yiannis, tells me.'

'Yiannis has been reporting on me?'

'Merely relaying his approval of you.'

'Oh.' She sounded surprised. 'He and his wife are very kind. They've been welcoming to me.'

'I'm glad to hear it,' he returned smoothly. It was all seeming very promising. She clearly liked living here, and she wanted the money. All that remained was whether she could stomach looking at him—and sharing his bed.

'And those are your only qualifications for a wife?' Milly asked.

'Yes.'

'Really?' She sounded cynical again. 'You don't care about your wife's likes or dislikes?

Her sense of humour, or her sense of honour? What about what kind of mother she'll be?'

Alex's mouth compressed. 'I don't have the luxury to care about those things.' Ezio's latest escapade had provoked a knee-jerk reaction in him to sort this, and quickly.

Milly was silent, and Alex watched her, noticing the emotions that crossed her face like ripples in water. Indecision, fear, but something else, as well. Something darker...guilt, perhaps, or grief. His proposition had struck a painful chord inside her. He was almost certain of it. 'And why an heir?' she asked at last. 'Isn't that rather an outdated concept?'

'It's a biological one.'

'Still.'

'I want to pass my business on to my child.'

'A son?'

'Or a daughter. It doesn't matter.'

She cocked her head, her eyes narrowing as she tried to make him out. 'Why?'

'Because if I don't,' Alex answered tersely, 'it passes to my stepbrother, who is likely to run it into the ground in a matter of months.'

'It's not like an aristocratic title, is it? Why should it pass to him?'

He drew a quick breath, forcing himself to relax as the memories bombarded him. Christos, looking so pale and weak, one claw-like hand extended towards him. *Begging* him. And Ezio, drunk in some nightclub, not even bothering to show up, to say goodbye to his flesh-and-blood father. 'Because my stepfather stipulated it in his will. The business was originally his, and he bequeathed it to me when he died. But he made a provision that if I should die without issue, it passes to my stepbrother.'

'That all sounds rather archaic.'

Alex inclined his head. 'Family ties are strong in this country.'

'Yet it's your stepfather,' Milly pointed out. 'This isn't about flesh and blood.'

'He was a father to me more than any other man was,' Alex answered gruffly. Emotion clutched at his throat, made it hard to speak. 'And the will is watertight. This is my only option.'

'What about adoption? Surrogacy?'

'As I said, time is of the essence. I'm thirty-six, and I want my child to be an adult when I pass the business on. Also, I believe a child should have a mother as well as a father. Family is important to me.' The words ignited a blaze of pain inside him, and he snuffed it out quickly. Coldly. The only way he knew how, to keep on living.

'What if I can't get pregnant?' Milly asked baldly. 'There are no guarantees.'

'You'd need to have a full medical check before we wed.' He shrugged one shoulder. 'The rest is up to God.'

'Would you want other children?'

He almost laughed at that. He knew she certainly wouldn't, not once she saw him. 'No, one will suffice. After that I will leave you alone.'

'Would I have to live on this island for the rest of my life?'

'You wouldn't be a prisoner, if that's what you are implying.'

'Would we have any kind of...relationship?' She spoke the word hesitantly, as if probing a sore tooth.

'We would treat each other with courteous respect, I should hope.'

'But beyond that?'

He couldn't keep from recoiling just a little,

just as he knew she would once she saw him. 'Is that something you want?'

'I... I don't know.' She shook her head, her teeth worrying away at her lower lip. 'This is all so unexpected. I can't even think straight.'

'Yet you are considering it?'

'I shouldn't.' She shook her head, expelling her breath in a gusty sigh. 'I don't even know why I am, if just a little. The *tiniest* bit.' It came out like a warning.

'The five million, perhaps.' He kept his voice light, inviting her to see the humour. To share it with him.

She shot him a look of wry amusement, and something small and warm bloomed inside him, something unexpected. When had he last shared a look with another person, even in the dark? 'Yes, that might have something to do with it.'

'I don't hold it against you.'

'And so you shouldn't, since you're the one who offered it. But perhaps I hold it against myself.' Her words came out sharply; the moment was broken, that small bit of warmth snuffed out.

Alex watched as Milly rose from the chair,

pacing the room, rubbing her hands together as if she were cold. 'No, this can't work,' she muttered, mostly to herself. 'I can't let myself, not like—' She broke off, shaking her head. 'No, I'm sorry. I can't. I won't.' She turned to him resolutely, her look one of both apology and determination. 'The answer is no, Kyrie Santos,' she said firmly. 'I'm sorry. I hope this won't affect our working relationship.'

Alex stared at her, refusing to betray his irritation and, yes, his disappointment, with so much as a flicker. And he did feel disappointed—more even than he'd expected. He could find someone else. He knew that. Yet her rejection stung, because that was what it was. It felt personal, even though he knew it shouldn't. And the laughable part was, he hadn't even turned the light on.

CHAPTER TWO

MILLY COULDN'T SLEEP. She lay tangled in her sheets, staring at the ceiling as moonlight slanted through the shutters of her window and silvered the tile floor of her bedroom. Since the abrupt ending of her conversation with Alexandro Santos this afternoon, when he'd more or less dismissed her from his study after she'd turned down his proposal, her mind had been reeling as she went over every surreal second of the bizarre interview.

I want you to marry me.

How could he have suggested such a thing? And how could she have been so treacherously tempted, even for a moment?

Milly turned over, thumping her pillow in a futile effort to find peace, or at least comfort. Her mind had not stopped zooming off in a dozen different directions since she'd left Alex; she'd kept herself busy, finishing the moussaka she'd been prepping for supper, sweeping the pool area, and paying a few bills, all the while wondering why he'd asked, what would happen now.

Would everything be awkward? Would he find a reason to fire her? She didn't want to lose this job. She was making three times as much money as she had been translating business documents back in Paris, and she liked the spacious villa with its beautiful flower-filled garden, the infinity pool, Yiannis and his wife, Marina, stopping by on occasion, the friendly village of Halki a short distance away.

She liked shopping among the quaint market stalls, a wicker basket looped over her arm as she examined lumps of feta cheese floating in brine, plump, red tomatoes, juicy olives.

She liked the little café with its rickety tables overlooking a dusty square where she sometimes sat and had a coffee after doing her shopping. She liked the quiet, starry evenings, the only sound the distant lapping of the waves. She liked the solitude, and feeling safe. She didn't want to leave here.

So why had she said no to Alex Santos' marriage proposal?

With a groan of frustration Milly rose from

her bed. She wouldn't sleep now. She slipped on her thin dressing gown and padded softly downstairs to the living area, opening the French windows as quietly as she could. Alex's bedroom was in the other wing of the house, one she only visited to clean, but she definitely did not want to disturb him now.

Outside the air was pleasantly cool, scented with bougainvillea and orange blossom. Moonlight glinted off the placid surface of the pool, giving it a ghostly feel. Milly wandered over to a wooden chaise and curled up on it, drawing her knees to her chest as she gazed out at the moonlit gardens. She let out a gusty sigh, tension that had been knotting her shoulders since Alex had said stay easing just a little.

She loved the peaceful solitude of this place—after a lifetime of the party or boarding-school scene, the quiet of her own company was a soothing balm, and the villa felt like a home, the first real one she'd ever had.

Five million euros. She couldn't stop thinking about it, about what she could do with that money. Pay for Anna's school fees. Pay for her university, buy her a house, keep her safe for ever. Money might not buy happiness, but it certainly helped…and the thought of finally having financial security, for her and for the one person she loved…well, after a lifetime of chaotic uncertainty, it was tempting indeed.

And so what if she married a man she barely knew? In her life, romantic love had been at best a joke, at worst a lie. She'd seen both her parents fall in and out of it with devastating ease, and her own brush with it had left her feeling more jaded than ever, still cringing in shame.

She didn't want that kind of relationship. She wouldn't take that kind of risk. At least Alex was honest about his feelings. That was more than she could say for Philippe.

So why not marry someone for the practical reasons? Alex's mention of an heir had sent a surprising ache of longing through her. A child of her own…someone to love, who couldn't be taken away from her. *Family.* She hadn't re-alised she was maternal in that way until Alex had spoken of it, but now, her knees tucked to her chest, she could almost imagine a baby nestled in her arms, the kiss she'd drop on its soft forehead. She'd be *such* a better mother than her own.

A sound from the house had Milly still-
ing, and then pressing against the back of
the chaise, trying to make herself invisible.
From the corner of her eye she saw Alex Santos make his way to the pool; he was wearing
nothing but a pair of loose pyjama bottoms
and moonlight bathed the sculpted muscles of
his chest in lambent silver, making her realise
just how impressive they were.

Milly's gaze rose from his chest to his face
and as if he could sense, not just her presence,
but her stare, he angled his head away from
her, his body going still.

'Couldn't sleep?' His voice was husky, somehow sensual, winding around her in the sultry darkness. Milly's arms clenched around
her knees.

'How did you know I was here?'

'You left the doors open, and I have good
eyesight.' He moved closer to her chaise, the
fabric of his pyjama bottoms whispering together as he moved, the muscles of his chest
rippling as the moonlight caught them. When
he was only a few feet away, his body still
swathed in darkness and his face angled away,
he spoke again. 'So why can't you sleep,

Milly?' He lingered on her name. 'Were you thinking about my offer?'

'Yes,' she admitted, because it seemed obvious. 'How could I not be thinking about it? It's the only marriage proposal I've ever received.'

'I'm sorry it wasn't more romantic,' he returned dryly. 'But I'm sure there will be others…that is, if you don't reconsider…?' He trailed off deliberately, and Milly swallowed hard.

'I shouldn't reconsider…'

'But you are.'

He sounded so certain, and why wouldn't he be? A handsome, powerful, wealthy man. And she was a plain little nobody. He'd probably expected her to jump at the chance. 'It's a lot of money,' Milly said on a shuddery sigh. 'And it would make a difference to me…and to someone I love.'

'Ah. Perhaps the most powerful reason of all.' Alex settled on the chaise opposite her, his face turned away, his gaze on the pool. 'And who is this person you love?'

'My sister. Well, stepsister, but she's as good as a sister to me. Better. The most important person in the world, the only person…' Milly's throat closed up at the thought of Anna and she blinked hard. 'I'd do anything for her.'

'Except marry me?'

'That's why I'm thinking about it.'

'It wouldn't have to be such torture, you know,' Alex said after a moment. 'I wouldn't bother you any more than I had to.'

Bother her? Was that really how he saw their potential relationship? And yet Milly felt reassured that her life wouldn't have to change too much.

'Most people want more from their marriage than that,' she said after a moment, and Alex arched an eyebrow.

'Most people,' he acknowledged, 'but not you, I think.' He turned so he could look her in the eye, although the darkness still hid much of his face. 'Am I wrong?'

Milly swallowed again, her throat dry as she struggled for words. 'I haven't thought about it all that much,' she hedged. 'I haven't…' She trailed off, her gaze on the silvery surface of the pool. 'I haven't had much experience,' she stated at last, determined to be frank. 'Of romance or romantic love. That kind of thing. And the experience I've had has put me off.'

'So here is the ideal solution.'

'Why don't you want romance or love in a marriage?' she asked hesitantly. 'I assume that's the reason for your business proposal?'

Alex shrugged. 'I don't see the point of it.'

'Of romance?'

'Or of love.' He paused. 'That kind of love. And neither, I think, do you.'

It was unsettling, how he seemed to reach right into her mind and pluck out her thoughts. What could he see in her face, even out here in the dark? What was she revealing without realising?

'I've seen it abused,' she answered at last, her tone careful. 'And I suppose I don't trust it very much. I'm not willing to take that kind of risk.'

'Good. Then I think we'd be an excellent match.'

She shook her head, an instinctive movement. 'It's not that simple...'

'Of course not. We can iron out the details as soon as you've agreed. I'm a reasonable man, Milly.'

The way he said her name made her shiver, although perhaps it was simply the cooling night air. 'None of this seems particularly reasonable, you know. We're talking about marriage. Having a *child* together...'

'It's eminently reasonable. Love is the outrageous thing, the ridiculous emotion that's meant to drive all our reason and ambition when it's so flimsy and ephemeral. The whole concept is absurd, insanity. Why would you trust your life to a fleeting feeling?'

'Yet people do.'

'But you're smarter than that, aren't you? As am I.'

She almost laughed at his arrogance, except she knew he was right. She *was* smarter than that. She'd wised up. 'See?' He smiled at her, the corner of his mouth curving upwards, his eyes—at least the one she could see—gleaming. 'We're a perfect match.'

'I haven't even seen your face,' Milly blurted, and although he didn't move, it felt as if he had. As if he'd gone even more still than he already was, every muscle taut and waiting, put on alert. 'Properly, I mean,' Milly clarified. 'We've only spoken in the dark. It's a bit... odd, you know. Clearly you're a private man, but...' Shouldn't she at least *see* the man she might marry?

'Yes, I am.' Alex was silent for a few seconds, seeming to draw into himself. 'Well, there is a reason for the dark.'

Milly gazed at him in confusion, squinting to make out his expression but it remained shadowed, unfathomable. 'Is there?'

'Yes, there is, but you might as well know it now. See what you might be agreeing to.' He walked quickly back to the French windows and in one quick movement he flicked on the outdoor lights. The terrace was bathed in a bright electric glow, and Milly blinked in the brilliance. Then Alex turned to face her, and a gasp rushed from her throat.

His face...

One side of his mouth quirked upwards. 'Perhaps now you understand a bit more of my reasoning for a convenient marriage?'

Milly sat transfixed, unsure whether to look away or keep staring. Would that be insulting? Unkind? In any case, she found she couldn't move her gaze. What had *happened* to him, since the photos she'd seen on the Internet had been taken?

'It's a shock, I know.' Alex spoke dispassionately, as if he didn't much care that half his face was ravaged in pink and white scar tissue, while the other half was entirely perfect, the coldly handsome man she recognised from his photos, made even more so by the damage on the other side. It was like looking in a cracked mirror, half crystal clear, half warped and broken.

'How…?'

'Fire.' The single word was clipped, dismissive. Milly knew instinctively he wouldn't say more, and she wouldn't ask. 'It puts off many a prospective bride, or so I imagine. I haven't deigned to find out. Perhaps it puts you off.'

'Your scars would have nothing to do with whether I agreed or not,' Milly said when she'd found her voice, but she feared she didn't sound convincing. It was just she was so *shocked*. Even with his insistence on privacy, the rooms shrouded in darkness, she hadn't suspected. Never guessed.

There hadn't been a whisper about it online, or even in the village, where most people knew him, or at least of him. Yiannis and Marina hadn't said a word.

'Very well, then.' Alex straightened where he stood, levelling her with a look. 'Will you marry me?'

Alex knew he should have given her time to adjust to the reality of his scars, but he felt too raw. He hated being looked at, despised the flicker of pity that inevitably crossed every person's face when they saw him in the light. So he made sure very few people did.

In the nearly two years since the fire, only a few trusted business advisors and staff had been able to look him in the eye. He didn't give anyone else the chance, not if he could help it. He entered his office from a private entrance, and, while there, he rarely left. Everything he could do from his office by phone or email, he did, and when he wasn't doing business he was keeping to himself, either in Athens or here, travelling by private jet or yacht to avoid the inevitable whispers and stares.

He had a few trusted staff who had seen his face and wouldn't talk, but he'd never had many friends and so he had even fewer now. As for lovers? What a joke. All in all, it was a lonely life, but it was the only one he could bear to live.

And yet he'd known this moment would come, when the woman who would be his wife would look on his face and shudder. He hated it with an intensity that made his fists clench before he made the choice, very deliberately, to flatten them out. He would not be that kind of man. Not like his father. It was a choice he made every day, deliberately, calmly, because he had to.

'I… I have to think,' Milly stammered, her gaze still tellingly transfixed by the scars that crisscrossed his entire right cheek, starting in his hairline and coming down to the corner of his mouth and quirking his lip upwards in a horrible half-smile he couldn't ever change. There were other scars too, ones she might not have noticed yet, cording the side of his neck and making a patchwork of white lines across his shoulder. 'It's such a big step…'

'Well, don't think too long,' Alex returned in a deliberate drawl, making sure to keep her gaze even though everything in him demanded he turn away. Hide. 'Because if you refuse,

I'll have to ask someone else, and as quickly as possible.'

'Do you have an alternative?' She sounded more curious than offended—or relieved.

He didn't, not yet, but he just shrugged. 'I have some possibilities.' None of the women of his acquaintance would agree to marry him looking like this, and he wouldn't want them anyway. Shallow, vapid creatures, caring only for appearances and wealth, and he had only one of those attributes.

No, he realised he wanted *her*, because she seemed sensible and trustworthy, and he had a feeling they could get along tolerably well, which was all he could ask for. All he would ever let himself want.

'Why me, though?' Milly pressed.

Looking at her, Alex knew he was fooling himself if he thought he wanted her just for those modest qualities. No, there was more to it than that. He wanted her, wanted her in the way a man wanted a woman. Desire was dangerous and foolish, and it made him feel exposed in a way he hated.

'You're here. You're suitable. You need the

money.' He bit each word off and spat it out. She flinched a little, but then she nodded.

'At least you're honest. I…appreciate that.' She sighed, turning away from him to stare out at the water. 'I love it here,' she said softly, and he tensed.

'That's a good beginning.'

'Is it? It doesn't seem nearly enough.'

'But if you don't want love in your marriage, why not this?'

'I feel as if I'm signing my life away.'

'You'd have every freedom.'

'Except the freedom to marry someone else.'

'True.' He paused. 'I would not countenance divorce. A child needs both parents.'

'Nor would I,' Milly returned sharply, with more force than even his tone had possessed. 'My parents are on their third and fourth marriages. I would *never* get divorced.'

Alex inclined his head. 'Yet another point upon which we agree.'

'I still don't know you. I don't know if you're kind, or trustworthy, or *good*.' Her voice throbbed with emotion. 'Shouldn't I know those things?'

Yes, of course she should, and he knew he

couldn't promise her any of it. He wasn't kind. He hadn't been trustworthy. As for *good...* 'I suppose you'll have to take my word for it.'

'And if we marry, and I discover your word is worthless? You...mistreat me...or lock me away...'

'Mistreat you?' He couldn't keep the offence from his tone, or a deep-seated conviction from shuddering through him. It was as if she were looking into his soul, and yet not seeing anything at all. 'I would *never* hurt a woman.' He'd never meant anything more, and yet she still seemed uncertain as she turned back to face him.

'I don't want to think you could do something like that, of course, but I don't know you, Alex. I don't know you at all.'

'Then ask me,' he bit out. 'Ask me whatever you want.' He stood there, bracing himself for whatever questions she fired at him, but she remained silent, gazing at him in helpless frustration.

'You make it sound like a job interview.'

'Of a sort.'

Another sigh and she nibbled her lip as she started to shake her head. He could feel her slipping away from him, like an ebbing tide. The scars had tilted the odds against him. Of course they had.

'I just don't think I can do this,' she said softly, her gaze sliding away from his. Her shoulders hunched; she looked guilty. 'I watched my mother marry for money, time and time again, and the results were disastrous... for her as well as for me and my sister. I can't be like her in that way. I won't let myself.' She paused, her shoulders hunched, her gaze averted as if she couldn't bear to look him in the face. 'I'm sorry.'

'Really, there is no need to apologise,' Alex returned stiffly. He wasn't going to argue with her; he certainly wasn't going to beg. 'Consider the matter closed,' he said, and then he turned and walked back inside the villa, staring blindly ahead all the while.

CHAPTER THREE

WHEN MILLY AWOKE the next morning, she knew Alex had gone. It was only a little past six, lemony sunshine banishing the last of the pearly grey light of dawn, but she knew all the same. She could almost hear the echo of the whirr of the helicopter blades signifying his departure; perhaps that was what had woken her up.

Quietly she slid out of bed and went to the window, opening the shutters fully to take in the breathtaking view of sun and sand, sea and sky. The blue-green waters of the Aegean Sea shimmered under the azure perfection of another summer's day. Inside Milly felt strangely hollow.

As soon as Alex had walked back into the villa last night, his body and gait both stiff with dignity and affront, Milly had questioned her decision—and not just because of the money. Yes, she could use the money, especially for

Anna's sake, but what if this was the only marriage proposal she ever received? More importantly, what if it was the best?

As Alex had sussed out, she was cynical and wary of such fanciful feelings as love and romance. If her parents hadn't put her off, her dalliance with Philippe certainly had.

Even now she could remember the mocking twist of his lips as he'd gazed at her. *'Do you honestly think I'd fall for a little mouse like you?'*

No, she wasn't going to go down that route again. So why not this? She wouldn't get duped or hurt, and she'd have financial stability, companionship of a sort, and even a child. After the financial and emotional turbulence of her entire childhood, who was she to scoff at those things?

Standing at the window, letting the sunlight stream over her, she wondered why she'd refused—even as she acknowledged why. Because her mother had married for money rather than love, and she never, ever wanted to be like her mother.

But this would be different, a little voice inside her persisted.

Would it? Another insidious voice mocked back. *Would it really?*

Turning away from the window, Milly went to shower and dress. She had a full day of housework ahead of her, and she needed to stop thinking for a little while. Blot out all the what-ifs and just *be*. Still, she wondered when Alex would return…and what it would be like when he did.

The house felt emptier than usual as she went about her work, sweeping and mopping and dusting. She put off doing the inevitable— cleaning Alex's bedroom, stripping the bed and washing his sheets. It had felt like any other room just days before, but now it was different. Perhaps she was.

After a solitary lunch reading at the kitchen table, she decided to put it off no longer, and in truth she was curious. Upstairs, down a separate corridor that held only his master suite and two guest bedrooms, she tiptoed towards his door, holding her breath, half expecting someone to pop out, something to *happen*. Of course, nothing did.

Milly pushed open his bedroom door and then stepped into the sparsely furnished room—a king-sized bed on a low dais with rumpled sheets and duvet, the indentation where his head had lain still visible on his pillow. There were no ornaments or knick-knacks, no photos or mementoes. There never had been, in her six months there.

The room was luxurious and as impersonal as could be, like something found in a high-end hotel. Milly began to strip the bed, her methodical movements belying the sudden thud of her heart, her dry mouth. Why was she being affected this way?

Unthinkingly she slipped off the pillowcase he'd used and pressed it to her face, inhaling an unfamiliar musky and very male scent. She was still holding it when her mobile phone began to vibrate, and she jumped like a scalded cat, dropping the pillowcase.

Her hands near to shaking, Milly slid her phone from the pocket of her jeans and glanced down at the screen. *Anna.* All thoughts of pillowcases and the head that had lain on them vanished as she swiped to take the call.

'Anna? Are you okay?' As ever Milly couldn't keep the anxiety from her voice as soon as she spoke with her sister. Her situation was so precarious, and she was so very young.

'I'm fine, Milly.' Anna's voice was quiet, a little sad. Milly knew she hated living with her father, Milly's stepfather—one of them, anyway—and Milly couldn't blame her. The situation was dire, and there was nothing she'd been able to do about it. Carlos Bentano kept custody of his only child more out of a cruel whim than any love or affection on his part.

'Good.' Milly walked away from Alex's bed, gazing out at the sparkling sea. 'I was hoping you could come visit here at the end of the summer,' she said, trying to inject a positive note into her voice, as if what she was suggesting could really happen. 'For a few weeks at least…'

'If he lets me,' Anna said quietly, her voice filled with doubt, and Milly sighed. Carlos Bentano and Milly's mother had married when she was fourteen and Anna just four. While their parents had been partying up with the last of their money, both penniless, minor aristocrats, Milly had been like a mother to Anna, only to be wrenched away from her four years later, after the inevitable and acrimonious divorce. In the intervening years, her contact with her stepsister had been all too fleeting; she'd seen her once or twice a year, if that, although not for lack of trying.

Carlos was just as likely to turn Milly away at the door of his dilapidated villa on the outskirts of Rome than let her in, and for no reason than it seemed to amuse him to be cruel. Meanwhile he hosted debauched parties, inviting all manner of dissolute reprobates into his home, and paid scant attention to his daughter by an earlier marriage—Anna's mother had died when she was a baby—and was indifferently negligent of her education. Milly was desperate to get Anna away from him, and five million euros would certainly help...

But she'd said no. She'd turned Alex Santos down, and right now, listening to her sister's voice wobble as she tried to be brave, Milly could not think why she had been so selfish.

'Why wouldn't he let you?' Milly protested as brightly as she could. 'It won't affect him, and he might like having the house to himself for a change.' But they both knew Carlos didn't care about that. 'How are things going, anyway?' Milly asked. She talked to Anna nearly every day, but, despite these daily conversations and reassurances that she was well, Anna was never able to allay her anxiety, a knot of tension that had lodged itself in her stomach six years ago, when they'd been separated.

'Okay,' Anna said on a sigh. 'He came back from the casino last night in a foul mood.'

'Oh, Anna…'

'I stayed out of his way, and he was gone again this morning.'

'But what do *do*?' Milly protested. She hated the thought of her sister drifting around like a ghost in that crumbling villa all by herself, day after day, but Carlos had already refused to let Anna come to Naxos for the summer.

'I read. Play music.' Anna was an accomplished violinist, and Milly loved to hear her play. 'It's better when he's not here. Last week…' She stopped, and unease ran its chilly finger down Milly's spine.

'Last week…?'

'It doesn't matter, Milly.'

'It does. Tell me, Anna, please.'

'Why?' Anna's voice trembled. 'There's nothing you can do.'

'What happened?' Milly demanded. 'I need to know.'

'It's nothing, really.' Anna sounded subdued now, which made Milly feel even more alarmed. 'He had some friends over, and they got drunk. One of them came into my bedroom…'

'What?' Horror clogged in her throat and she tasted bile. The thought of some drunken lout in her little sister's bedroom made her want to run all the way to Rome, as fast as she could. 'Anna, what happened? Did he…did he try anything?'

'No, no, he went out again. He apologised, even…'

Milly felt herself breathe a little easier, but she still felt suspicious as well as deeply afraid. She didn't think Anna was telling her everything, and what if next time the drunken guest wasn't so accommodating? What if her sister was in more danger than Milly had ever realised or feared? With her honey-blonde hair and big blue eyes, Anna was lovely, and just becoming a woman. She would be irresistible to some of Carlos' debauched friends.

'Do you have a lock on your door?' Milly

asked. 'Because I think you should lock it. Every night.'

'I've put a chair under the knob since then. Really, it's okay, Milly.'

But it wasn't at all okay. Milly breathed in deeply, willing herself not to cry. She didn't want to make Anna feel worse. 'I'm so sorry this is happening to you, Anna,' she said softly. 'This isn't at all how I hoped your life would be like.' When she'd been little, Milly had promised to take care of her. Vowed to always protect her. And now she was powerless.

She sent money when she could, and she had a savings account in Anna's name, but there was so little she could do.

And yet with five million euros you could do so much more. You could bribe Carlos for custody, even...

'It's not your fault, Milly,' Anna said. 'And actually I was calling for another reason.' She paused, and Milly steeled herself, hoping there wasn't more to worry about. 'A space has opened up at the academy,' Anna continued hesitantly. 'I just got the email this morning.'

'The academy...' Milly's mind raced. She knew Anna had been dreaming of going to the prestigious music school in Rome for several years, but there had been no space, and, more importantly, no money. Carlos would never agree to pay for anything, and Milly couldn't afford the fees, even with her generous salary.

'That's wonderful, Anna, but—'

'I know it's a lot,' her stepsister continued in a quiet, intense voice. 'And you can't possibly pay it all, but I've arranged to give music lessons to some neighbours. It's not much, but it would help—'

'Oh, Anna.' Milly bit her lip. She doubted her sister could make nearly enough teaching violin to make up the difference, but she couldn't bear to disappoint her and put a stop to her dreams. 'What does Carlos say?'

'I haven't told him, and I don't plan to. He doesn't care where I go to school, and he might refuse just because he could. Besides, he doesn't have the money, and if he did, he certainly wouldn't spend it on me.'

'But...'

'I can forge his signature. I've had to before, when he's forgotten to sign forms and things. I'd leave and return home the same time every day, not that he notices. It could work, Milly. I'm sure of it. It's just the money...'

'I'll see what I can do.' Tears pricked Milly's eyes as she thought of her sister desperately trying to make this dream work, and all on her own strength. She was so young, and yet far too old for her years. Milly couldn't bear to think of the debauched scenes Anna must witness in her father's home, when Carlos had his horrible friends over. And when she thought of one of those amoral men looking at Anna, coming into her bedroom...

She had to do something.

'Thank you, Milly,' Anna said earnestly. 'I really appreciate it.'

'I can't make any promises,' Milly felt compelled to warn, even though she wanted to promise Anna everything. 'Send me an email with the details of the fees, okay? And I'll try to make the numbers work.' Although she doubted they would...*not unless she had five million euros.*

'All right.' Anna hesitated. 'The only thing is, the space won't be open for ever. The *principale* said I needed to send my deposit by the end of the week.'

'The end of the week—' Milly couldn't keep the words from coming out in a squeak of dismay.

'I'm sorry. I never dreamt a space would come up in time for me to start...'

'Send the email,' Milly repeated firmly. 'I'll look into it this afternoon, and if I can swing the fees, I'll wire the deposit as soon as possible.' Although it made her stomach sink to think of it. How would she be able to afford such a thing? And yet she knew she wanted to. Desperately.

How desperately?

That little voice continued with its sly whispers after Milly had ended the call. Desperately enough to marry Alex Santos? That would solve all of Anna's problems. *Do you really want to keep her safe?*

Milly scrunched her eyes shut, trying to block out that whisper, but it did no good.

Well, do you? the voice mocked. *Do you?*

'There is a woman here to see you, Kyrie Santos.'

Alex frowned as he listened to the disembodied voice of the receptionist on the intercom. 'A woman? I have no appointments. You know that.' His voice was sharp with recrimination. All the staff at his headquarters in Athens knew he didn't take unscheduled appointments. He didn't want prying eyes, ever. No one saw him while he was here; he had had a private entrance installed with a lift that went directly to his penthouse office. His door was always closed.

'Yes, I know, sir…' The woman sounded apologetic as well as uncertain. 'But this woman insists…'

'Insists on seeing me?' Alex repeated in disbelief. Who on earth could it be? It didn't matter. 'Then you can simply tell her I am not—'

'Insists that she is your fiancée,' the woman corrected in an embarrassed rush. 'I'm sorry, sir. I didn't know if…' She trailed off uncertainly while Alex frowned at his intercom, trying to process what he'd just heard. His *fiancée*?

Something far too like hope flared in his chest. *Milly.* It had to be her. She'd changed her mind…and she'd come all the way to Athens to tell him? He was surprised as well as both gratified and curious. 'Send her in,' he said gruffly, and then he rose from his chair and stalked to the window, trying to control his wayward emotions.

Since leaving the villa—and Milly— they'd been in a frustrating ferment. He didn't want to care about her refusal. He didn't want to feel the rejection, and yet he did. He'd been stewing over it for the better part of two days, telling himself it didn't matter even though he knew it did.

She was just a housekeeper, after all, and yet he'd wanted her. He'd wanted her to marry him, because rather surprisingly, considering how quick his decision to ask her had been, he realised he wanted her and no other. He desired her with a strength that surprised him; he'd spent the last few nights lying awake imagining his hands on her skin, his mouth... But of course their wedding night, if it happened, would be an exercise in endurance rather than an experience of passion.

With his gaze on the window and his back to his office, he heard the door open and then click softly shut, followed by a quick shudder of breath that made the hair on the nape of his neck stand up. She sounded as if she were steeling herself, and she probably was. He knew from experience it didn't get any easier to look at him. Every time he glanced in the mirror it was a shock.

'Kyrie Santos,' she said quietly.

'Alex,' he reminded her. He didn't turn from the window; no need to remind her of his scars. She was undoubtedly thinking of them already.

A heavy silence ticked on for several taut moments. 'I've…reconsidered your offer,' Milly finally said, her voice matter-of-fact and determined. 'If it's still open.'

Alex's gaze rested on the skyscrapers of Syntagma Square, his heart thudding hard even as he kept his voice measured, almost toneless. 'It is.'

'Then I'm here to say I will marry you… Alex.' Her voice held a tremor of emotion, perhaps fear. Was she scared of him? Or just repulsed by his scars? Maybe both, and for good reason. He hadn't given her any real reason to respond otherwise.

'Why have you changed your mind?' he asked. 'As a matter of interest?'

She took a quick, telling breath. 'I had more time to think about it.'

'And what did you conclude?' He couldn't keep a sardonic note of cynicism from entering his voice.

'That five million euros is a very good deal,' Milly answered after a moment, her voice ragged with honesty. 'And it will help my sister immeasurably.'

She sounded resigned—resigned to her fate, to him. She was signing her death warrant, and why? For the sake of her sister, of course. There was no other reason. He would be something she had to endure to get what she wanted. Had he ever expected anything else? Of course he hadn't. That was the deal he'd offered. That was what they were both getting. There was no reason to feel stung by it now. No reason at all.

'Very well,' Alex replied coolly. 'Then I will have the prenuptial contract drawn up immediately. Once you've signed it, we can be married immediately.'

'Immediately…' She sounded a little dazed by the prospect.

'There is no time to waste. I told you I wanted an heir. I'll arrange for you to have a medical examination tomorrow morning.' He heard her gasp but he didn't care. So what if he'd been blunt, even crude? It was the truth.

'But…but there's still so much to discuss…'

'Such as?'

He heard her swallow, and in his mind's eye he could picture the working of her pale, slender throat, see the widening of those pansy-brown eyes, the rise and fall of her chest. 'Lots of things. How it's going to *work*, mainly, and…and what precautions will be in place…?'

'Precautions?' The word came out sharp.

'I'm putting my life in your hands,' Milly retorted, her voice just as sharp as his. 'I need guarantees, Alex. Safeguards…'

'Very well. Then I'll put those in place.'

'Can't you turn and look at me?' she burst out, sounding both exasperated and emotional. 'I hate having a conversation with your back.'

He pressed his lips together, biting back the instinctive reply. *I didn't think you wanted to look at me.* He wouldn't lower himself by saying such a thing. Instead he turned around to face her, schooling his face into an expression of bored disdain.

'Here you are. And here I am.'

'Yes.' She gazed at him steadily, and he saw

her gulp, her gaze darting to his scars and then back again. Her face was pale, her eyes huge. 'So now what?'

'Now we discuss the terms. The safeguards you mentioned.' He strode from the window and sat in one of the leather club chairs in front of his desk, gesturing for her to take a seat in the other. 'Shall we?'

'All right.' Milly walked over to the chair and sat in it.

Just two days ago they'd been in his study at the villa, talking about terms in theory. And here they were again, talking about them in reality. Everything had changed because she had agreed to become his wife. They *would* be married. He did not feel as triumphant as he'd thought he would…especially as Milly's gaze moved over his face, sliding away from the scarred side, and her fingers trembled before she knotted them together in her lap. 'So…?' Her tongue darted out to moisten her lips. 'Why don't you tell me what you suggest?'

'I suggest we marry immediately,' he answered with a shrug, purposely keeping his tone clipped, almost bored. 'As I said before.

I can have the prenuptial contract drawn up by tomorrow, and we can be married the day after. I will have the marriage licence rushed.'

Milly squared her shoulders. 'And what would the prenuptial agreement state?'

'That you will receive five million euros, which will be repayable to me should we divorce.'

'Repayable?' She blinked. 'That's harsh. What if *you* divorce me?'

'I won't. But, to address any worries you might have on that score, I will have it put into the contract that you will be given an additional five million euros should I wish to divorce you.'

She shook her head as a shiver went through her. 'This is all sounding so cold.'

'Clinical, perhaps, but not cold. It's a business arrangement, Milly. We both know that.'

'Yes, but…are we ever going to get to know each other, even a little? Talk properly?'

Alex suppressed a shaft of impatience. 'We're talking now.'

'*Properly*, I said. Enjoying each other's company as…as friends, if not anything else. Have some sort of companionship, especially if

we're going to be...to be *parents*.' She choked
on the word, her eyes huge. 'And what about
that? What about how we raise our child?'

'We can discuss that in due course.'

'But don't you want to know me at all?
Or have me know you? I mean, even just a
little...' She trailed off, searching his face—
and for what?

He stared at her for a long moment, wondering if she really wanted some kind of friendship—and why. Did she really want to get to
know him, or was it just a salve to her con-
science, because she felt guilty for agreeing to
such a businesslike marriage? It was all pointless anyway, because he had no desire to get
to know her. No wish whatsoever to make this
more complicated than it needed to be. More
emotional, more dangerous. Desiring her physically already felt like a step too far, a need he
knew he shouldn't nurture.

And yet, despite all that, he could see the
sense in a conversation, at least. Besides, he
had a conference call in five minutes.

'Very well,' Alex said at last. 'I will arrange
for you to stay at the Hotel Grande Bretagne
for the next few days. Tonight we can meet for

dinner and…talk.' His lips twisted, the scar pulling tight across his cheek. 'Get to know each other as you seem to wish…and agree on all the terms.'

CHAPTER FOUR

MILLY STARED AT her reflection in the gilt-framed mirror in wondering disbelief. Could this really be happening? Everything felt surreal, from the moment Alex had ushered her out of his office and an assistant had escorted her to the limousine waiting by the kerb.

It had been only a few minutes' drive to the luxurious hotel just off the other side of the square, and then up to the presidential suite, the most expensive and elegant accommodation in the hotel. Milly had wandered around the gracious rooms with their antiques and art—a dining room, living room, two bedrooms, both with en suite bathrooms nearly as big—wondering if this was what the rest of her life was going to be like. It seemed impossible.

Although her parents were both titled, they'd lived in shabby elegance, if that, barely scraping by on what was left of their inheritances;

Milly was used to draughty mansion flats with leaky pipes and the heat cut off, or third-rate boarding schools in distant, remote locations with stern teachers and freezing showers.

Once she'd left home, she'd lived even more modestly—a cramped box room in a dilapidated student house in Edinburgh, and then a shoebox-sized studio in Paris. This was something else entirely, and it made her feel... strange. Was this what she would become used to?

But she hadn't been left alone to dwell on it for very long; she'd barely walked through the rooms before hotel staff were knocking on the door, ushering in a three-course lunch under silver domes and then, a short while later, a personal stylist from a nearby boutique wheeled in several suitcases of clothes, with instructions for her to pick whatever she wanted. Milly was overwhelmed.

And while it was rather fun to dine on lobster salad and caramel profiteroles, and even more so to pick out several simple and elegant outfits, it was also unsettling. What did Alex Santos want in return?

She knew the answer, of course. *An heir.*

And that thought made her tremble, a shiver that started deep inside, in the core of her being, and spread out to the tips of her fingers and toes.

She could hardly believe she'd agreed to marry a man she barely knew, and yet she felt she'd had no choice. After ending the call with Anna, Milly had realised she would do whatever it took to make her sister safe and happy. And if marrying a stranger was the price she had to pay, so be it. It could be a lot worse.

She believed—or at least she hoped—that Alex Santos was a decent man. The knowledge that she had no real basis for that assumption settled heavily inside her.

At least she would have an opportunity to find out more about him before she signed any agreements or spoke any vows. Milly knew she was resting a lot on a single evening's conversation, but it was all she had. And hopefully, by the end of the night, she'd know more about the man she'd agreed to marry. Perhaps she'd even like him. That would be as solid a foundation for marriage as any she could hope for, and certainly better than what fools called love.

Her lips twisted grimly as she remembered how carelessly Philippe had used that word. *'Chérie, I love you. I fell in love with you the first time I saw you...'*

And like a besotted fool, she'd believed him. She'd wanted to believe him, because she'd wanted her life to be different from her mother's... Angelique Dubois, the ageing beauty who fell desperately in love, or seemed to, all the while having her eyes on the prize.

Her mother had married for money thrice over, and was now living in Los Angeles with her D-list celebrity husband, a man whose claim to fame seemed to be how many times he could check himself into rehab. Milly had never met him, and she hadn't seen her mother in years, except occasionally in the back of tawdry gossip magazines, usually in one of the smallest photos on the society pages.

She glanced in the mirror again, wishing she looked a little more...elegant. She'd taken a shower and spent an age styling her hair and doing her make-up with the high-end beauty products she'd been provided with, but in the end she'd wiped it all over and dragged a brush through her hair because she'd looked like she was trying too hard. She'd looked like her mother, painted with fake gloss, a shiny veneer that chipped all too easily. She never wanted to be like that.

And so here she was, dressed in a burgundy wrap dress of softest jersey, her hair in simple waves about her shoulders, not a lick of make-up on her face. She knew she wasn't beautiful, so there was no point even trying. Alex Santos was not marrying her for her looks, that much was sure.

From the front of the huge suite a door opened and then clicked shut, and Milly's heart stuttered. It was him, she knew it. She sensed it, even though staff had been going in and out all afternoon. It was as if the air around her had changed, and another shiver started in her core and radiated out.

'Milly?' His voice was terse, his footsteps echoing on the marble floor. Milly turned from the mirror, smoothing her palms down the sides of her dress as she took a steadying breath.

'Here,' she called, and stepped out of her bedroom into the hallway. Alex stilled just a few feet away, his gaze training on her, not a flicker of emotion on his face. It was still jarring to see his scars—half of him so very beautiful, and the other half pulled and twisted beyond recognition. She tried not to react, but she could tell she'd failed by the way his mouth tightened. She would get used to them eventually, she was sure. She wasn't *bothered* by them, by any means; they were just surprising, the contrast so stark.

'You look nice,' he said gruffly, and dropped his briefcase by the hall table.

'Thank you.' She let out a nervous little laugh. 'I've been ridiculously pampered since I arrived here. I feel like Cinderella.'

'And when will the clock strike midnight, do you think?' he asked sardonically as he tugged at his tie.

Milly watched him uncertainly, her gaze transfixed by the sight of his long, lean fingers pulling at the silken knot around his throat. He pulled it free with a snick of cloth and tossed it aside before undoing the top two buttons of his shirt. Again her gaze was helplessly drawn to his fingers, and the bit of bronzed skin he exposed—the hollow of his throat, the hint of his muscles. He was a beautiful man, and in a strange way the scars emphasised that. Her breath fluttered in her throat and she swallowed. Hard.

'What do you mean?' she finally asked when she'd managed to regather her senses. 'Do you think I'm going to change my mind?'

'I wouldn't be surprised if you did.'

'I won't.' She spoke firmly, determination firing her words. 'I've made up my mind and I won't change it. But perhaps it is you who will change yours.' Although she hoped he wouldn't. She'd wired all her savings to pay for the deposit on Anna's school fees, and she needed the five million euros by next week to pay the rest.

'Hardly,' he scoffed, and then turned to stride into the living room. After an uneasy pause Milly followed him.

She stood in the doorway and watched as he unstoppered a decanter of whisky and poured himself a finger's worth. 'I've ordered our meal to come shortly.'

'All right.'

'So.' Alex walked to an elegant chair patterned in striped silk and sat down, the tumbler of whisky dangling from his fingers, his face angled away from her so she could only see his unmarked side. 'Tell me your terms.'

'I don't actually want to talk about terms. Not yet.' Carefully Milly crossed to the sofa perpendicular to him and sat down. 'I just want to talk.'

Alex lifted the glass of whisky to his lips and took a long swallow. 'Talk?' he repeated tonelessly. 'About what?'

'About each other. I want to get to know you, Alex, if just a little, and have you get to know me. I… I don't want to marry a stranger. Even business deals can be amicable.' She pleated her fingers in her lap, her heart jumping around in her chest. 'Can we do that?'

Alex took another sip of whisky as he considered Milly's question. Could she get to know him? Could he get to know her? It all sounded so innocuous, so sweetly innocent, and yet…

He was darkness inside, and if she saw that… if she *felt* it…she might change her mind. She almost certainly would. Never mind the scars on his face, there were worse things for her to discover, things he was able to hide. Yet refusing might make her reconsider. He had to walk a very fine line between friendliness and honesty, darkness and light.

'All right.' Alex forced a smile to his lips, and felt the familiar tug of his scar on the corner of his mouth. 'Let's talk.'

Silence pooled between them, stole the air. Alex waited it out, watching Milly as she struggled with what to say, where to look.

'Where did you grow up?' she asked at last.

'Here in Athens. Next?'

Her lips twitched, her eyes flashing with annoyance at his abrupt manner, but the truth was he didn't know how else to be. He'd long ago lost the ability to make small talk, if he'd ever had it. He'd learned to watch himself from an early age, and since the fire he'd become even more private and remote. He could not imagine changing. He had neither the desire nor the ability.

'Do you have any brothers and sisters?' Milly asked.

He clocked the present tense and answered it accordingly, already feeling far too raw, exposed by these seemingly innocent questions. 'Just the stepbrother, Ezio, from whom I'm trying to save the business.'

'You were close to your stepfather?' Milly recalled, and everything in Alex tightened. Already this was too difficult. Too much. His fingers clenched on his glass, knuckles aching.

'Yes. Now let me ask you some questions.'

'All right.' She settled herself back against the sofa, her slender hands resting on her knees. She looked lovely in the simple wrap dress, the burgundy colour picking up the dark honey strands in her hair, the gold glints in her eyes. Alex's gaze took in the simple tie at the waist that held the dress together and he imagined giving it one firm tug and seeing it come undone.

Heat flared inside him, dangerous and alarming. How could he desire her with such fierce need? He'd picked Milly James as a prospective wife because she was convenient, not beautiful. And she wasn't beautiful, in the conventional sense. If anything, she was exceedingly plain, with her brown eyes and hair, her slight figure. And yet right now he wanted her more than he'd ever expected—not just as a wife, but as a woman. That was unfortunate, because he doubted very much that she wanted him in the same way.

'Where did you grow up?' he asked, shifting to ease the ache that had started in his groin.

'All over. London, Paris, Buenos Aires for a bit.' She gave a small shrug. 'A few other places.'

'That sounds rather exotic.'

'If you like.'

She sounded guarded, which made him curious. 'Is there a particular place you'd call home?'

'Your villa on Naxos,' she replied, surprising him. 'It's an oasis of peace compared to some of the other places I've lived.'

'That's good to hear.'

'Yes.' She glanced away, something in her shuttering. It seemed she had secrets as well, or perhaps just pain. He felt a flicker of empathy, the last thing he'd expected to feel.

'And your stepsister?' he asked after a moment. 'Where does she live?'

'Rome.'

'Not too far, then. Do you see her often?' As far as he was aware, she hadn't taken off any time since being in his employ.

'As often as I can, but her father doesn't always allow it.'

Alex frowned. 'Why not?'

'Because he likes to be cruel?' Milly shrugged, glancing back at him with bitterness in her tone and pain in her eyes. 'He's a capricious wastrel, and he enjoys nothing more than being petty and cruel simply because he can. I've arranged a visit many times and at the last moment he slams the door in my face.'

Alex stiffened at the thought of a man being so wantonly wicked. He knew what capricious cruelty looked like, what it felt like, and he hated it with a fierce and deep-seated passion. 'Can't your sister get away to see you?'

'She's only fourteen, and she's afraid of him.' Milly's arms wrapped around herself, almost as if she were keeping herself together. 'Five million euros will help to protect her.'

'How, if your stepfather is as capricious as you say?' Making the point was hardly in his favour, yet he couldn't keep himself from it. The last thing he wanted was for her to regret their marriage more than she had to.

'I can pay for her school fees,' Milly said in a low voice. 'That will make a big difference. And if I offer Carlos a financial incentive, he might be willing to let Anna visit me more often.' Her gaze flew to his face. 'That would be all right, wouldn't it? To have her visit...'

'Of course,' he said tersely. 'I'll make sure to stay out of the way.'

She looked surprised, but then she nodded. Of course, she wouldn't want him there, scaring her sister.

'Who is this Carlos?' he asked. 'As a matter of interest?'

'Carlos Bentano. My mother's third husband, ex for the last six years.'

'Ah.' There was a wealth of meaning, a world of bitterness in her simple statement. He remembered her saying how she would never want to divorce. 'And what about your father?'

'He's on his third marriage. My mother has moved on to her fourth, although I doubt they'll last very long.' She shook her head, her hands now clenched in her lap. 'I don't see either of them very much at all.'

'It sounds like it was a difficult way to grow up.'

'Not much fun,' she agreed, and then deliberately made herself relax. 'Not the way I'd choose to raise my own child, certainly.'

'Our child,' he reminded her, and watched

her eyes flare—with alarm, no doubt. He needed to remind her of the purpose of their marriage—to produce an heir, and as soon as possible. Just in case she might forget that a wedding night was most certainly part of the deal, and as many nights thereafter as it took for her to become pregnant. After that he would leave her alone.

That persistent ache intensified, and his fingers itched to tug at that sash and watch the dress come undone. He pictured himself standing before her, spreading his hands to span her waist, feeling the warm, silky flesh come alive beneath his palms.

Then he pictured her flinching beneath his touch, averting her face. No, their wedding night, or any other encounter, wouldn't happen like that. It would be as businesslike as the rest of their marriage, because neither of them wished to suffer through anything more.

'Yes, our child,' she agreed softly as she lowered her gaze, her head bent.

'Should we talk about the terms now?' Alex asked curtly. They'd had enough of getting to know each other, it seemed.

She looked up, her momentary surprise replaced by stoic composure. He wished she didn't look as if she had to *endure* him quite so much, but he knew he couldn't expect anything else. 'All right.'

'So the terms of the contract will be simple. In exchange for five million euros, you will marry me, stay faithful to me, and agree to share my bed until you become pregnant.'

She swallowed, the sound audible. 'And how often am I to share your bed?'

The way she said it made him think she wished to as little as possible. Alex hesitated, surprised by his own reticence to make this aspect of marriage as cold and clinical as the rest of it. And yet of course it had to be. 'Three times a week, unless it is during your monthly courses.'

'My...' Her face began to flush with colour. 'All right.'

'Do you wish to suggest something different?'

'No...' She swallowed again, and then let out a shuddery little breath. 'No.'

'I will endeavour to make it as pleasant as possible,' Alex said, his mouth twisting into a sardonic grimace. 'I appreciate the difficulties, of course.'

She didn't answer, which bizarrely annoyed and even hurt him. He had to stop *caring* so damn much. 'Is that all satisfactory?'

'And what about when I...when I am pregnant? If I am? What will happen then?'

'Then I'll leave you alone.'

'For...for good?' She looked startled. 'You're sure you don't want more children?'

For a second he imagined it, pictured a houseful of them—babies, toddlers, teens. Crowded around the table. Laughing in the garden. A fantasy. 'As I said before, one will suffice. After you have become pregnant and given birth, there won't be any need for us to continue the...arrangement, although of course we will still stay married.'

She nodded slowly, seeming to absorb that statement—and not to mind it. 'And I'll raise the child...our child...on Naxos?'

'Yes, until he or she is of an age to need more appropriate schooling. But those things can be negotiated at a later date. The important thing is to have the initial terms set down so we can move forward.'

'I can hardly believe we're doing this so quickly...' She shook her head, and Alex cut across her, determined not to give her the opportunity for second thoughts.

'It's how people have been doing it for centuries. There is no reason to think we won't both be happy.'

He'd meant to sound dismissive, but she cocked her head, her gaze moving over him slowly, taking him in, scars and all. 'Happy?' she repeated softly. 'Are you happy, Alex? *Will* you be happy?'

There was far too much sorrowful knowledge in her question and in her eyes, too much damned pity. 'I will be happy with the arrangement,' he told her shortly. 'That is enough.'

It wasn't until after he'd said it that he realised how revealing his answer was. A knock sounded on the door, and Alex called out in Greek for the member of staff to leave their meal in the hall, as they did not wish to be disturbed.

'Dinner is here,' he announced once the staff member had left, the door clicking shut behind him. He rose and strode towards the entrance hall of the suite. 'I hope you're hungry.'

'I am, even though I had an enormous lunch. I forgot to eat breakfast this morning, because I was in such a rush to get the ferry.'

'I didn't expect you to come to Athens,' Alex remarked as he wheeled in a trolley full of silver-domed dishes.

'I didn't know when you would be back in Naxos, and I wanted to see you as quickly as possible. Because of Anna.'

He glanced at her sharply. 'What is the urgency with your sister?'

'She's found a place at a prestigious music school in Rome. She was on the waitlist, and a place has come up at the last moment. She's desperate to go—it will make a big difference to her, to attend.'

Alex frowned. 'Will her stepfather forbid it?'

'He won't even know. At least, that's how Anna is hoping it will all play out. But I needed to secure the deposit by the end of the week.'

'The end of the week...'

'Oh, don't worry,' Milly said quickly. 'I've paid it out of my savings. I'm not asking you to pay for anything...' She bit her lip. 'I mean, I'll pay for her school fees out of, you know, the settlement.'

'I see.' She'd had even more reason to want that money—the only reason she would ever go through with something like this, clearly. She needed to provide for her sister, who, in a few days' time, would be as good as his sister-in-law. *Family.* He didn't want Milly to be scraping and saving in order to provide for what would be *his* family.

'I called her this afternoon,' Milly said quietly. 'To tell her I'd sorted the fees. She was so pleased.'

'And did you tell her you were to be married?'

'No.' Her lashes swept her cheeks as she lowered her gaze. 'I didn't want her to feel...'

A pause, and Alex filled it in grimly. 'Guilty? Because you've had to sell yourself in order to provide for your sister?' Milly stared at him uncertainly, clearly not knowing what to make of his comment, or why he'd made it in such a grim voice. And why had he? Everything was happening exactly as he'd intended it should. There was nothing to feel dissatisfied or unsettled about. Nothing at all.

CHAPTER FIVE

'DO YOU HAVE ANY QUESTIONS?'

Milly stared at the lawyer's bland face, her mind spinning. Did she have any *questions*? She glanced back down at the sheaf of papers spread on the desk in front of her, the typewritten text swimming before her eyes. She didn't even know where to begin.

'Miss James?' The slightest hint of impatience touched the lawyer's urbane voice.

'I think it should all be quite clear,' Alex interjected. He'd been sitting on the sofa in the lawyer's spacious office, silent and practically glowering, which Milly suspected was his usual look, at least when he had to appear in front of someone. The lawyer had seemed unsurprised by Alex's scars, but still kept sneaking looks at them, which Alex clearly noticed.

Milly took a deep breath as she tried to marshal her thoughts. She'd listened to the lawyer for the last hour as he'd outlined the terms of the prenuptial contract, but she'd hardly taken any of it in. She could still barely believe she was here, that she was thinking of doing this. She *was* doing this.

Last night, after their brief chat, she and Alex had eaten dinner mostly in silence. The food had been delicious, but it had begun to taste like ashes in Milly's mouth because she wanted conversation, not comfort. She wanted companionship, at least in a small degree, and as the evening had worn on she'd feared Alex would not be able to give it to her. Didn't *want* to give it to her, which was worse.

She'd made a few attempts, asking him why he chose to settle on Naxos—because it was convenient—and what his business was actually about—buying and selling property. She'd given up after a while, which she suspected was what Alex had wanted. Milly hadn't expected hearts and rainbows from him; of course she hadn't. But a little conversation wouldn't have gone amiss. She told herself it was better to know what to expect, and at least he wasn't attempting to flatter her the way Philippe had. Still, it felt like cold comfort indeed.

After dinner he'd returned to his apartment,

curtly informing her that a limo would pick her up at nine for her medical exam, and then take her afterwards to his lawyer's office where they would go over the prenuptial agreement.

Then Milly had spent a restless night wondering what on earth was she doing even as she knew she wasn't going to change her mind. She couldn't, for Anna's sake. For Anna's happiness.

But this morning she was awfully tempted. First, she'd endured the most clinical medical exam she'd ever had at a private medical clinic, squirming in indignity and shame as the doctor had asked her questions about her period, her sexual history, her fertility.

When she'd left the office, her cheeks still scarlet with mortification, Alex had been waiting in the back of his limo. She'd blushed harder when he'd informed her that the doctor would email him the report. So now he would know her periods were regular, she'd never had an STD, and even that she was a virgin. Milly couldn't bear to meet his eye, but he didn't seem eager to meet hers, either.

He'd ushered her quickly into the limousine, and since then he'd seemed intent on ignor-

94 GREEK'S BABY OF REDEMPTION

ing her as much as possible. He looked devastatingly attractive in his steel-grey suit, his eyes piercing and blue, his dark hair the perfect foil to his crisp white shirt. The lawyer was obsequious in the way he studiously avoided looking at Alex's scars, and she could tell it annoyed Alex. It annoyed her as well.

She was already getting used to them, seeing the scars simply as part of who he was. Perhaps because she'd been around such superficial beauty for so long, she found she didn't mind them in a way he seemed to think people did. Her mother had chased physical perfection with spa days and surgery, expensive ointments and endless make-up, and in the end the beauty was nothing more than a glossy veneer. At least Alex's scars were real.

'Are you going to sign it, Milly?' Alex asked, his voice cutting through her jumbled thoughts. 'Or not?'

'Sorry...' She'd been simply staring into space for the last minutes, and she saw now that the lawyer was impatient, Alex annoyed. She reached for the heavy, expensive-looking fountain pen the lawyer had laid on the table next to the contract and uncapped it, her heart starting to thud.

She hadn't been able to take in all the terms the man had gone through, but she knew enough to understand the gist of what she was signing. Sort of.

She'd receive the five million euros as soon as they were wed. They were to have regular conjugal relations until she was confirmed pregnant. She would live on Naxos, but be free to travel to Alex's homes in London and Athens. Any other trips needed to be approved by him, although he'd assured her he would be reasonable. It felt a little bit like prison, a gilded cage, and yet, considering what she was getting, nothing seemed that unreasonable.

And yet…in the end, she was still selling herself for money. Did a wedding ring really make it respectable?

'Milly…' Alex said her name like a warning, and she closed her eyes.

She couldn't back out now. *For Anna.* She was doing this for Anna. Her mother had married various minor aristocrats so she could fund her extravagant lifestyle. Milly was doing it for the person—the only person—she loved. It was completely different. It had to be.

Wordlessly she bent her head, the contract's type swimming in front of her, and signed her name. Milly felt as if she'd just opened a vein and dripped blood onto the snowy white documents.

'There we are,' the lawyer said smoothly and picked up the contract, shuffling the papers into a neat pile. 'I believe that concludes our business for today.'

'Thank you.' Alex turned towards the door, and Milly followed him, her stomach churning.

What had she done?

For Anna. This is for Anna.

'That wasn't so bad, was it?' Alex asked her once they were safely ensconced in his limousine, the tinted windows hiding them from the world.

'I suppose not.' Milly's voice was shaky and she found she had to blink back tears. She hated feeling so raw and uncertain; she'd revelled in the quiet solitude of the last six months, the safety of them, and now she felt as if she'd just upended her entire life. She had no idea what to expect. Nothing felt certain or safe. Were they really going to be married *tomorrow*?

'Don't look so devastated, then,' Alex said, his voice a sardonic drawl. 'I promise I will make as few demands on your time as possible.' He turned away from her to look out of the window, and Milly tried to speak past the lump forming in her throat.

'Is that what you think I want?' He merely shrugged, and she made herself continue. 'I'm not expecting some sort of fairy tale, Alex. Of course I'm not. I wouldn't even want one, because I know they're not real.'

'Then we don't have a problem.'

'It would just be nice to be *friends*,' Milly persisted, her voice turning a little ragged. 'Right now it feels as if you can barely tolerate me.'

'I can tolerate you?' He let out a harsh laugh. 'Let's be honest with each other, Milly, if we can't be anything else.'

She gazed at him in confusion, wishing he would at least look at her. 'What do you mean?'

'You're the one who can't tolerate me,' Alex said flatly. 'And I don't blame you for it.'

She gaped, unable to frame a reply for several taut seconds. 'Is that really what you think?' she finally managed to gasp out. He'd always seemed so cold, she had trouble believing he could think that. Alex lifted one shoulder in a negligent shrug. *'Look at me,'* Milly demanded. 'If we are to be married, at least look at me.'

He swung around to face her, his eyes glittering like blue fire—or maybe ice, because his expression was cold. Cold and furious. 'Are you sure you want to look at *me*?'

He held her gaze, and Milly did not look away. She didn't even blink. 'Is this about your scars?' she asked evenly, willing her voice not to tremble. She could feel the heat rolling off him, inhaled the citrusy scent of his aftershave that awakened her senses. 'Do you honestly think I'm so shallow? Why would you be willing to marry me if I was?'

'Shallow or not, I'm not very pleasant to look at,' Alex returned flatly. 'Fact.'

'Isn't beauty in the eye of the beholder?' Milly asked softly, and Alex rolled his eyes.

'How can you even say that with a straight face? You don't find me beautiful, Milly.'

She hesitated, sifting through her jumbled thoughts, and then chose honesty, painful as it was. 'No, I don't,' she agreed, and something flickered across Alex's face before his expression closed off completely. 'But not because of your scars. Because of how…how *cold* you're being. It feels as if you're choosing to distance yourself, and that's not how I want to start our marriage, even if it is one that is based on business.'

Alex was silent for a long moment, staring at her. Their faces were so close she could see the dark glint of stubble on his freshly shaven chin, the icy blue of his eyes piercing her like an arrow. She inhaled the musky smell of his aftershave again, and her heart tumbled in her chest.

Then Alex eased back, turning his head away from her in a deliberate movement. 'Too bad,' he said, and neither of them spoke again.

So she thought he was cold. Alex gazed dispassionately at his reflection in the mirror— full on, so he could see both the beauty and ugliness, the scars and the smooth skin. Dr

Jekyll and Mr Hyde in the flesh—and in the soul. His face, he feared, was a reflection of who he truly was. Hiding the darkness. Pretending to the world that he was only half of who he was. That he didn't hurt the people he loved. That he didn't destroy them.

And she thought he was simply cold. Well, cold was better than cruel. Cold was fine—because it kept them both safe. And Milly would just have to learn to live with it, because he didn't know how to be anything else. From his childhood he'd learned to stay distant from other people, out of self-preservation, and that had only been exacerbated since his accident. Eventually she would accept how he was, and realise it was better this way. It had to be.

In any case, he saw the way she looked at his scars. She might say they didn't matter, but of course they did. How could they not? He'd seen the pity in her eyes, the way her gaze darted away, and that told him all he needed to know.

He turned away from his reflection and glanced at his watch; he was meeting Milly in a few minutes to take a limousine to his private yacht docked at Piraeus. From there they would travel to Naxos, where they would be married.

Alex had been planning on a civil ceremony at the city hall here in Athens, but yesterday, after they'd signed the prenuptial agreement, after that taut confrontation in the limo, Milly had asked if they could marry on the island, in a church.

'I know it's a business deal,' she'd said with quiet dignity, her chin tilted at a proud angle, 'but it doesn't have to be businesslike in every particular, and I would like to marry in a church and say my vows before God.'

'Wouldn't you be saying them before God in any case?' Alex had drawled, and she'd merely gazed at him steadily, waiting for his answer, refusing to be baited. He'd felt shamed by his seeming pettiness; the truth was the whole ordeal of being with her, having her look at him, having her want to *know* him, even in the smallest degree, left him feeling raw and exposed, as if yet another layer of skin had been peeled back to reveal the agonising nerve-endings underneath. He had enough scars already. He didn't need any more.

'Please, Alex,' she'd said. 'This is a small request.'

Small to her, perhaps, but not to him. She had no idea what awaited him on Naxos, why he'd been back only once since the fire, and he was hardly going to tell her now. And so he'd agreed, even though he dreaded the thought of facing the villagers of Naxos, because he didn't want to have to explain and, in truth, something in him wanted to please her, which was absurd yet true. The small smile of thanks she'd given him when he had agreed had lightened his heart a ridiculous amount.

Milly was already waiting in the limousine when he left his flat; his driver had picked her up at the hotel before fetching him. Alex slid onto the leather seat, his thigh brushing hers before she inched away. He wondered if she would shrink away like that tomorrow night, when they were in bed. He thought it likely, but she would simply have to grit her teeth and bear it as she held up her end of the bargain.

'I didn't know you had a yacht,' she remarked as the limo pulled away from the kerb. 'You came to Naxos by helicopter.'

'I don't have time usually to travel by sea, but it does tend to be far more relaxing.' He paused, and then, somewhat to his surprise, decided to make the effort of conversing. 'Do you like sailing?'

'I don't know, I haven't been, really.' She smiled self-consciously. 'The only boat I've been on is the ferry to Naxos.'

'It is?' He frowned. From what she'd said of her parents, he'd surmised they were fairly well off, and she'd said she had lived in several cosmopolitan cities. 'I'm surprised.'

'Are you?' She shrugged. 'I never had the opportunity.'

'Yet you've lived in Paris, in London, in Buenos Aires.'

'What does that have to do with sailing?'

'I simply thought you would have had a variety of life experiences.'

She paused, her face drawn in reflective and even sorrowful lines. 'I suppose I've had certain experiences, but in their essence they've all been the same.'

'How?' The word came out abrupt, and she raised her eyebrows, a faint smile playing about her mouth even though her eyes still looked soft and sad.

'You want to get to know me now?'

'I'm curious.'

She shrugged. 'My mother found me to mainly be an inconvenience. She sent me to boarding school when she could afford it, and left me at home when she couldn't.'

Alex frowned. 'And what about your father?'

'They divorced when I was five. I rarely ever saw him.'

It sounded miserable—about as miserable as his childhood, and yet as far as he could tell she hadn't had the loving care of a stepfather the way he had been blessed to have. 'Were any of your step-parents decent people?' he asked. 'Besides Bentano?'

'I wouldn't call them parents, really,' Milly answered after a moment. 'They certainly didn't see themselves in that role.'

Which told him everything he needed to know, and left him feeling oddly unsettled, although he couldn't say why. They didn't speak again until the limousine pulled up to the dock at Piraeus, and Alex ushered her towards the gleaming white superyacht.

'This is yours?' Milly's eyes widened as she took in all fifty metres of the impressive structure.

'It belonged to my stepfather,' Alex answered as he took her hand to help her aboard. One of his staff, paid to be discreet and blank-faced, stepped back. 'He used to host parties on it, for business.'

'And you don't?'

'No.' Not any more.

She gazed at him uncertainly, their hands still clasped, her slender fingers resting on his. 'Because of your scars?' she asked quietly, and he cringed at the pity he thought he heard in her tone.

'Yes, but also because I am not much of one for parties. Never have been.'

'You seem a very private man,' Milly acknowledged as he led her into the main living area, a luxurious, wood-panelled room with several leather sofas scattered about the plush, ankle-deep carpet. 'Were you always so?'

'Yes, I suppose.' He'd had to be. He turned away from her. 'Would you like something to drink? It will take about six hours to get to Naxos. We can be there by dinnertime, and then the wedding is scheduled for tomorrow at midday.'

'All right,' Milly said, her voice sounding quiet and a little sad. 'And yes, please, could I have some water?'

Alex snapped his fingers and one of his staff, one of the few he trusted to see him, stepped forward. 'Sparkling water and a whisky, please, Petros.'

'Very good, sir.'

Petros withdrew, leaving them alone. The yacht shuddered beneath them for a few seconds and then began to glide through the water.

'Are we going already?' Milly looked surprised, and a little excited. Alex recalled what she'd said about never having sailed.

'Yes, would you like to see?' He opened the French windows that led out onto one of the yacht's many decks, this one private, with a couple of rattan sofas and chairs. Ahead of them the Aegean Sea stretched out, a simmering, undulating blanket of blue-green.

Milly stood with her hands on the rail, her hair blowing back from her face, as she gazed out at the sea. She reminded Alex of the statue of winged Nike—courageous and proud. The thought made some forgotten ember flicker to life in him, something he thought had long ago crumbled to ash.

He imagined, for one piercing second, how things could be different. How they could talk, and laugh, and then go back inside and tumble into bed, spending the six hours to Naxos very pleasantly occupied. But of course none of it was going to happen like that. He was a fool even to dream of it, to let himself want it for so much as a moment. He'd *never* let himself want that kind of life.

'Are you looking forward to returning to Naxos?' he asked.

'Yes.' She turned to give him a small smile, her eyes crinkling at the corners. 'I really am.'

Alex watched her, noticing the glint of gold in her eyes, the dimple in her right cheek. For a second she looked happy, and it made him realise how worried and withdrawn she'd been before. It also made him realise that he liked seeing her happy, and the possibility that he might be able to be the person who made her so, even just for a brief moment, felt intoxicating. Impossible.

She was smiling because she was returning

to Naxos, to the place she felt was home. It had nothing to do with him. It never would.

'Our drinks are here,' he said, and walked back inside.

CHAPTER SIX

MILLY STOOD AT the railing, watching as the smudge of grey-green came closer. Naxos. *Home.* She'd spent the six hours of their journey exploring the superyacht, prowling about its empty, opulent rooms feeling both anxious and dissatisfied. Alex had locked himself in his study as soon as they'd finished their drinks, claiming he had to work. Milly had a feeling he would be doing that a lot, and she told herself it was better that way. Better not to complicate things with anything so arbitrary as emotion.

That was what she'd agreed to. That was what she'd expected.

She breathed in the sultry, salty air, her heart lightening just a little as she imagined being back at the villa, among its familiar, comfortable rooms. *Safe.* And soon Anna would be too, God willing. Milly hoped Carlos would see reason and let her stepsister visit her on occasion, maybe even every holiday…

The thought of having Anna with her sent a smile spreading across her face and happiness blooming inside her chest. It would all be worth it then. The wedding, *the wedding night…*

Milly's heart juddered in her chest at the thought. She could not picture their wedding night beyond some hazy montage, like something out of a film, all soft focus and swelling violins. Of course, it couldn't exactly be romantic, and she would be a fool to expect or even want that. But would Alex become tender, once they were alone and intimate?

She had so little experience, and he knew that, thanks to the medical report. Would he be patient? Gentle? She hated the thought of being so vulnerable and exposed with a man who viewed that part of marriage in as businesslike a way as any other, and yet she feared that was exactly how it would play out… despite the way her heart somersaulted in her chest when she imagined him touching her. Kissing her…

Her whole body felt heated and she lifted her

face to the sea breeze, willing the cool air to fade the telling flush from her cheeks. Never mind the wedding night, what about the wedding? She didn't even have a wedding dress, or a bouquet, or a veil. She had never been the kind of little girl to daydream of wedding dresses and fairy tales, but there were a few basics she thought she would have liked to have on the day, no matter how it had come about.

Now she told herself not to mind. She wasn't having that kind of wedding, that kind of marriage. It was still worth it, for Anna's sake. It had to be.

From behind her she heard the sliding door open and then Alex stepped out; his very presence sent a shiver skittering along her skin, a visceral reaction she could not suppress but hoped he didn't notice.

'We're almost there.'

'Do you moor the yacht at the villa?'

'Yes, have you never been down to the dock?'

'No, I haven't. I've seen it, but I've never had any reason to go down there.' Alex's island property encompassed over fifty acres. Milly had stayed in the villa and gardens mainly, with a few walks among the scrubby brush and olive groves that surrounded the place, but she hadn't ventured to the dock, which had been empty while Alex's yacht was moored in Piraeus.

'I'll give you a full tour, later,' he said, and she turned to him with a surprised smile.

'Will you?' She was pleased by the thought, but when she looked at Alex, he looked as if he regretted extending the invitation.

They were drawing closer to the dock, the villa rising above it on its clifftop, the dazzling white walls and blue-shuttered windows silhouetted against a lavender twilit sky, the sun a half-circle of burnt ember sinking behind the hills. Milly narrowed her eyes; someone was waiting on the dock.

'Who is that?' she asked, because she was always alone at the villa, save for Yiannis and his wife Marina, who came several times a week to do the gardening and maintenance around the place, and lived in Halki.

Alex didn't answer, and she glanced at him, wondering what was going on. His expression was suspiciously bland, as if he knew something but wasn't saying. 'Alex? Have you… have you hired another housekeeper?'

'Another housekeeper?' He looked surprised.

'I thought you might have…because…well, because…'

'Because you're going to be my wife?' he filled in. 'As it happens, I haven't hired someone else, but you can hardly continue in my employment, Milly, when you will be married to me.'

'I suppose not.' She saw the sense in it, but she liked her role at the villa.

'If you like, you can hire a housekeeper, when the time comes. You'll spend more time here than I will.'

'I'd rather just do it myself.'

He frowned, but then shrugged. 'Very well. It will be your choice.'

Which should have been a relief, but it also felt like a rejection. He didn't care what she did with her own time, in her own place; of course he didn't. She had to stop expecting something else, something deeper or kinder. She'd known what this was going in and she'd convinced herself she could live with it, even that it was what she wanted. Why was it so hard to accept? Why did some contrary part of her keep looking for more, even as she told herself she didn't want it?

'So who is that waiting on the dock?' she asked, and then her breath caught in her chest as they came close enough for her to glimpse the familiar dark blonde hair, the slender figure. 'It isn't…' But as the yacht drew closer to the shore, she knew it was. 'Anna,' she breathed, and then she shouted it, waving frantically. 'Anna… *Anna!*'

Tears sprang to Milly's eyes as her sister caught sight of her and started waving back just as frantically, jumping up and down in her excitement.

Milly turned to Alex, blinking back tears, overwhelmed with emotion. 'You did this,' she exclaimed as tears spilled over and she dashed at them. 'How…how on earth did you arrange it?'

He shrugged. 'Bentano can be a reasonable man when he has the right incentive.'

'But how…?'

Another shrug, the hint of a smile at the corner of his mouth that lightened Milly's heart even more. 'He's an ass, but he saw sense.

Anna can stay here until she starts school in three weeks.'

'What...?' Milly breathed the word, hardly able to believe she had Anna for three whole weeks, and, even more poignantly, that Alex had thought to arrange it. *How* had he managed it? And when? 'I don't know what to say.'

'There's no need to say anything.'

'But there is. This was so kind of you, Alex. I wasn't expecting...' She paused, unsure how to continue. She hadn't been expecting him to do nice things for her. It seemed to go beyond their business arrangement, and yet he had, and without any hint or hope from her. It overwhelmed her. It humbled her. And treacherously, it gave her hope that their marriage could be something just a little bit more than the cold and clinical deal he had first suggested. Not much more, of course, because neither of them wanted that. But a *little.* 'When did you arrange it?' she asked. 'How was there time?'

'I spoke to Bentano this morning, and fortunately for him he saw sense almost immediately. She flew on my private jet, and she arrived in Naxos just before us. Yiannis picked her up at the airstrip.'

What had Alex said or done to induce Bentano to agree? Milly couldn't even imagine it, but she knew it must have been something big. And he'd done it for Anna...and for her. 'Thank you, Alex,' she said, her voice throbbing with sincerity.

And then, because that didn't feel like enough, Milly stepped closer to him and put her arms around him in what was meant to be a simple hug, but immediately felt like something she shouldn't have done.

Alex stiffened in shock, but not before their bodies collided, Milly's breasts against the hard wall of his chest, her legs pressed to his so she could feel the outline of every powerful muscle. Heat flared within her, a white-hot pulse of sensation that jolted through her entire body and made her take a stumbling step back, shocked by the intensity of her feeling. *Her desire.* It ignited everything inside her, so she felt as if she were burning up. Had Alex registered her response, and was horrified by it? The thought was mortifying.

As Alex watched her step back, his expression closed right up, like the snapping shut of a fan. Milly realised she was already used to it, that emotional distancing he seemed to accomplish effortlessly. Clearly she'd stepped across a major line. 'Alex…' she began, but she had no idea how to explain what she'd been feeling, at least not without embarrassing herself. Her body still pulsed with a molten heat she'd never felt before, not even with Philippe. And Alex didn't seem to want it from her now.

'Milly!' She turned to see Anna calling to her from just a few metres away as the yacht was moored at the dock. *'Milly!'*

'I'm coming,' she called, and when she turned back, Alex had disappeared.

As soon as Milly left the yacht, Alex still nowhere in sight, Anna practically jumped on her. Laughing, she hugged her sister, so grateful to be with her once again. It had been far too long.

'I've missed you so much,' Milly exclaimed as they both wiped away tears. 'So, so much.' It had been nearly a year since she'd last seen her sister. 'I think you've grown a couple of inches, Anna.' Her sister definitely looked a little older, and even more beautiful with her honey-blonde hair and bright blue eyes. There could be no more men stumbling into her bedroom, of that Milly was certain.

'I can't believe I'm here.' Anna looked both emotional and thrilled. 'This place is amazing, Milly. And you have so much to tell me. You're getting *married*? How come you didn't mention that on the phone, huh? That's pretty big news.'

'Ah. Well.' Milly smiled weakly. 'It's hard to explain…'

'What's there to explain? Your fiancé sounds *so* nice. He insisted on flying me in his private jet.' Her blue eyes rounded comically. 'It was *incredible*. There were staff who just kept feeding me. I had the biggest ice-cream sundae I've ever seen.'

'Wow.' Milly let out a shaky laugh; her emotions were all over the place, from that sudden, surprising hug with Alex, to that terribly awkward moment afterwards, and now her sister with her for three whole weeks. Plus she had to explain her imminent wedding to her, and the reason for it. It all felt like too much. Her head and heart both ached, and, strangely, she wished Alex were here, helping her through this moment, although would he even be much help? Or would he just tersely tell her to get on with things, with that stony look on his face?

'Why don't we head back to the villa?' she suggested, taking Anna's arm.

'Where's Alex? I want to meet him.' Anna craned her head, looking for Milly's fiancé, but he still wasn't anywhere to be seen. Milly suspected he'd absented himself on purpose, and would continue to do so, a prospect that gave her a little pang of sorrow as well as one of relief. It was easier this way, but it still felt lonely.

'I think he's working,' she improvised. 'He's very busy with everything at the moment.'

'He must be.' Anna dropped her voice to a theatrical whisper. 'Milly, he's *mega*-rich!'

'Yes, I know.' Milly let out another little laugh. Like her, Anna had grown up on the fringes of an aristocratic world yet with no money. Like Milly, Anna was used to second-rate schools and draughty, crumbling buildings; neglect and genteel poverty were the standards by which she'd been raised. Milly had had six months to get used to the luxury of the villa; Anna was seeing it all for the first time.

'So how did you meet?' Anna asked as they walked up the winding, rocky path towards the house. 'Was it love at first sight?'

Milly thought of Alex's curt proposal in his shadowy study, and didn't know whether to laugh or cry. How on earth could she explain the business deal she'd made to her starry-eyed fourteen-year-old sister? She almost wished Alex had told her about Anna's arrival, so she could have prepared what she'd say. How she'd explain.

'It's a long story,' she said as they stepped inside the villa, the thick stone walls providing a blessed coolness. 'Have you eaten? Let me get you something…'

'I'm stuffed from all the food on the plane.' Anna flung herself on one of the squashy sofas in the living area off the kitchen. 'This place really is amazing. So, long story. Start from the beginning, because I want to hear everything.'

'I don't know if I can.' Milly tried for a light laugh as she poured them both glasses of water, handing one to Anna before pressing her own glass to her hot cheek. Anna looked at her, her eyes narrowing.

'What are you not telling me?'

'I haven't even started yet,' Milly protested. 'I haven't told you anything, Anna, obviously.'

'You know what I mean.'

Of course she couldn't fool her sister. Anna was ten years younger, but far too wise for her years, and she and Milly had always had a connection, even when they hadn't seen each other. It was like an invisible wire, drawing them together, binding them tightly even when they'd been hundreds or thousands of miles apart.

'You do love him, don't you?' Anna asked uncertainly, and now she sounded far too young. Milly looked away. '*Milly.* Why are you marrying this man if you don't love him?'

'He's a good man, Anna.' At least she hoped he was. Only a good man would arrange for her sister to visit, surely? It felt like evidence, proof, but hardly enough to build her life on... which was exactly what she was doing. Because she had to.

'How long have you known him?'

'Six months.' Which was more or less true, even if she'd only seen him for the first time a handful of days ago. 'He's my employer,' Milly explained. 'This villa is where I've been living as housekeeper.'

'That sounds like it could be romantic.' Anna's forehead crinkled. 'Falling for the boss... *is* it?'

What should she do? Say? Milly hated the thought of lying to her sister, but the truth felt too unpalatable to share. She couldn't burden Anna with the knowledge that she'd done this for her sake. It wouldn't be fair. 'It is, a bit,' she finally said. 'At least, it could be. The...the truth is, Anna, we're marrying as a sort of... business arrangement.'

'Business?' Anna sounded horrified. 'But, Milly—'

'But amicable too,' she continued quickly. 'Alex needs a wife, for, um, work reasons, and so...' She couldn't find a way to finish that sentence.

'So?' Now Anna looked horrified, as well. 'But what do you need, Milly? What do you get out of this?' She leaned forward, her eyes huge and swimming with tears, her expression beseeching. 'Please, *please* don't tell me you did this for my sake. For money. I couldn't bear it if you did.'

Milly stared at her helplessly and then did the only thing she felt she possibly could. She lied.

Today was his wedding day. Alex gazed at his reflection, wondering if anyone had heard he was on the island, that he was getting married. Would any of the villagers who had known him and Daphne be waiting at the remote chapel where the wedding was to take place? What would they think of his ravaged face, his presence here?

He'd avoided Naxos since the fire, unable to bear the place where he'd once been so happy, and when he had come here only a few of his staff had seen him. They were tight-lipped and loyal, and so no one from his past here knew what had happened to him. All they knew, he realised with a tightening in his gut, was that their darling Daphne had died. Daphne and Talos. And they would blame him, because it was his fault.

How would they react when they saw him? Would they sneer? Hiss? Spit? He wouldn't blame them for any of it. Nothing one of the villagers could say could be worse than what he'd said in his own mind. What he lived with every day. Two of the people he'd loved the most had died, and it was his fault entirely. The scars he bore were remarkably little punishment, considering.

And it seemed fitting, and somehow just, to walk among the people who had loved Daphne, to let them see his shame. To feel their hate… even on his wedding day. But perhaps no one would come to the chapel where they were to be married, a short distance from Halki. Perhaps the gossip hadn't spread of his marriage; perhaps they didn't care.

Squaring his shoulders, Alex turned away from the mirror.

He'd avoided Milly and Anna since their arrival yesterday, closeting himself in his study and missing meals. His fiancée and her sister would want some alone time, and he had no desire for Anna to flinch from his scars along with his bride-to-be.

Then yesterday evening Milly had slipped into his study and asked him to at least meet her sister before their wedding day. He'd said yes, because he realised it would be better for Anna to see his scars now and not in the church. But when he'd made an appearance on the terrace that evening, the setting sun turning the sea to a shimmering plate of gold, Anna greeted him without a flicker or quiver. Clearly Milly had prepared her for what he looked like, and he didn't know how to feel about that.

Upon examination, he realised he felt an irritating mixture of gratitude and hurt, which didn't make any sense. It was the same kind of ferment of emotion he'd experienced when Milly had hugged him and then stepped away so quickly—desire and disgust, hope and disappointment. He couldn't blame her for her reaction, and yet it still nagged at him, like a paper cut that wouldn't heal.

After trying to feel numb for so long, it all felt like too much. He didn't understand why he was responding to everything, why the simplest smile or gesture made him feel scraped raw. It wasn't supposed to be this way; he wanted, he *needed* to stay in control. Instead he felt edgy and irritable.

Even now he could remember the soft and pliant warmth of her body pressed against his for a few torturous seconds and his body ached with memory and desire. She'd jumped away from him as if she'd been scalded—or repulsed.

Well, tonight they would be closer still, but he would do his best to make it as brief as possible. That was the least he could do for his bride…perhaps the only thing.

Alex strode outside the villa, the bright summer sun hitting him in the face with a blast of unforgiving heat. Yiannis, acting as his driver, gave him a smile in the rear-view mirror as Alex climbed into the back of the car.

'You are ready, Kyrie Santos?'

'Yes. As ready as I'll ever be.'

'She is a good person, I think,' Yiannis ventured. Yiannis had been with Alex for over a decade; he'd been there at the fire, had helped to drag him out. He was one of the few people Alex trusted implicitly, and he knew Milly better than Alex knew her himself.

'Yes,' Alex answered tersely as he thought of Milly, her shy smile, those pansy-brown eyes. 'I think she is.' Unlike him.

They did not speak again as Yiannis drove him the few kilometres to Saint Panormitis, the tiny little red-roofed chapel set among the rocky hills outside Halki, the barren sweep of land meeting the bright blue horizon.

It was a lonely place, yet no less beautiful for it, the chapel huddled among the scrub and brush, its whitewashed walls dazzling under the azure sky. No one was waiting outside save the priest and the witnesses, two of Alex's staff in addition to Yiannis. He glanced around for Milly, but he couldn't see her anywhere, and with a lurch of panic he wondered if she hadn't turned up. What if she'd backed out at the last moment? He wouldn't even blame her, not really. Five million euros wasn't nearly the good deal she thought it was.

Yiannis touched his elbow. 'Miss James has gone into Halki,' he said quietly. 'For flowers.'

Relief pulsed through Alex even as he realised he hadn't considered any of the usual details involved in a wedding—flowers or a dress or the traditional party afterwards. Did Milly want those things? Should he have put some consideration into their business arrangement?

No, of course he shouldn't have. Realisation jolted through him, strangely unwelcome. Of course they wouldn't have those things. Why dress up what it was they had, put the plain truth in frills and lace? Milly had told him she was wary of love, cynical of romance, and he was the same. There was no need to pretend otherwise now, simply because they were making vows.

And then he turned and saw her. His heart seemed to stop in his chest as she crested the hill, her hair blowing loosely about her shoulders, a bouquet of tiny white star-like flowers and trailing ivy clasped in her hands. She wore a dress of ivory silk, the cut simple and lovely, with cap sleeves and an empire waist, the lace-edged hem brushing her ankles. Anna walked a little bit behind her, looking youthful and pretty in a pink sundress, and grinning with such obvious happiness that Alex felt jolted.

This almost felt like a *real* wedding. Which, of course, it was. And yet…he felt wrong-footed, *wrong-hearted*, as Milly walked towards him, a smile like a promise on her face, in her eyes. She was looking at him as if she *felt* something. She held out one slender hand, the other holding her bouquet.

'Shall we walk in together?'

Alex stared at her helplessly, so surprised by this moment, by her and even by himself. It felt far too important, as well as too sweet. The cold business deal he'd imagined was morphing into something else entirely, a couple on a hill, holding hands and making promises.

Anna, he saw, was still beaming at them as if she thought they were truly a man and woman in love. And for a single, blazing second, Alex could almost imagine that they were. That this was simple. 'All right,' he said, and he tucked Milly's hand into his, liking the feel of it there, snug and warm and safe.

Then together they walked into the little church.

CHAPTER SEVEN

SHE WAS MARRIED. Milly hadn't actually spoken any vows or made any promises, but the Orthodox priest had spoken for them, and they'd exchange crowns of laurel and shared a common cup, traditions in the church that Milly didn't completely understand but still seemed sacred.

She knew what they'd done was binding. She'd felt it in her soul, as if she'd just jumped off a cliff and now was soaring in the sky, unsure whether she'd continue to fly or plummet to the earth like Icarus with his waxen wings. How had Alex felt about the ceremony? When she'd looked into his eyes as they'd drunk from the same cup, she hadn't been able to tell a thing.

He hadn't spoken throughout the ceremony, and nor had she, but before they'd walked into the church, he'd almost looked...well, it was hard to know how he'd looked, considering how closed he was generally, but for a second he'd seemed…*moved*. And that had filled her with a sudden, buoyant hope that she was afraid to examine too closely. She wasn't going to fall in love with him or anything stupid like that, just because he'd been a little bit nice to her. She was going to keep this businesslike, because that worked for them both.

And yet…that moment had given her pause. Made her wonder if this odd agreement could turn into something else, something more like friendship. She would never wish for more than that. She wouldn't let herself.

Now they walked out of the church in silence, blinking in the bright sunlight, a married couple, although Milly still had no idea what their marriage was going to look like. *Or their wedding night.* The thought made her heart flutter with both anticipation and alarm.

As she stepped outside, it was so bright that she was blinded for a moment, but then she heard applause, and, when she finally blinked the world into focus, she saw a scattering of villagers on the rocky hillside, about two dozen men and women, all of them clapping, their gazes trained on Alex, their expressions strangely sober. She glanced back at Alex, and saw he looked as startled as she did.

Yiannis, his driver, said something to Alex in Greek, but Milly couldn't make it out. She had no idea what was going on. Who were these people?

Then Alex spoke. *'Efharisto,'* he said, a word Milly knew. *Thank you.* But then he said something else that she didn't understand, and the villagers all started shaking their heads. Anna glanced at Milly in confusion, but she just shrugged. She had no idea what was happening, or who these people were. Did they know Alex simply because he had a villa on the island? It seemed deeper than that, their silent stares both compassionate and convicting, as well as weirdly intense.

'Come on,' Alex muttered. 'Let's get in the car.'

'What about all these people...?'

'They've got what they came for.'

She frowned. 'And what was that?'

'To see me.'

'See you...' She shook her head. 'But why were they clapping for you?'

'They were clapping for us. For our marriage.' But Milly hadn't quite got that feeling. They had been looking at Alex, not her. It had felt more personal than mere congratulations. But her husband clearly was not in the mood for answering questions, for he took her by the hand and led her towards the waiting car. She climbed in, and Alex followed, then Anna. In silence Yiannis drove them away.

'So congratulations,' Anna said brightly once they'd left the chapel, the car hurtling down the hill towards home. 'That was a beautiful service.' She beamed at Alex, who looked entirely nonplussed, as well he should. Anna was acting far too cheerful. 'I hope you're going to celebrate today.'

He slid Milly a guarded look. 'I hadn't thought of it.'

'Well, I have,' Anna announced. Surprise flickered across Alex's face and then was gone, replaced by a cold, closed look Milly already knew well.

'Have you?' he remarked in a neutral tone.

'Yes. It's not much, but you are married and I think you should celebrate.' She gave him a challenging look, which Alex met, and Milly wondered how to intervene. How to keep her sister from spinning fairy tales, and annoying her husband.

Yesterday, when Anna had asked her if she loved Alex, Milly had spun a tissue of lies about how she'd fallen in love with him as soon as she'd been hired, gazing at him from afar until he'd asked her to marry him for business reasons.

She'd told Anna she'd said yes to his proposal because she wanted to be with him so badly, and she hoped he'd return her feelings in time, as he got to know her. Anna had bought the whole silly story from first to last, her eyes starry as she'd exclaimed how romantic it all was, while Milly had felt more and more wretched for lying to her sister.

'He must have some feelings for you already, Milly,' Anna had exclaimed. 'Why else would he ask you, you and not some socialite, to marry him?'

'I was convenient.' Already Milly had seriously regretted spinning the stupid story, but how could she tell Anna the truth? Her sister would feel horribly guilty that she'd forced Milly into a loveless marriage, even if Milly had been the one to make the choice. And it

was her choice. She wouldn't let herself regret it.

'Still. He *will* fall in love with you, Milly, in
time. Head over heels.' Anna's eyes had spar-
kled. 'I'll make sure of it.'

'Anna...' Milly had started in warning, but
her sister had been on a romantic roll, determined to make the day special when Milly
knew it wasn't—and her husband-to-be didn't
want it to be. That morning Anna had insisted
on going into Halki so Milly could buy a wedding dress and flowers.

Amazingly in the tiny village they'd found
a wonderful dress in a dark and narrow little
shop, one that fitted Milly perfectly, and felt
like fate. When he'd heard about the wedding,
the local grocer had picked flowers from his
garden and given them to her for free, kissing
her on both cheeks as he'd wished her health
and happiness.

Milly had been torn between getting caught
up in others' excitement, and a growing sense
of dread that Alex wasn't going to like any of
these romantic details. In fact, he'd probably
hate them.

He'd seemed dangerously nonplussed by

Anna's breathy sighs and approving smiles during the short ceremony, her sister clearly imagining a fairy tale where there so glaringly was none.

Now the truth of their marriage was being revealed, as Alex stalked towards his study. He'd already plucked the laurel crown from his head and tossed it aside carelessly as Milly watched him, trying not to feel hurt even though she knew she'd save her crown, as well as her bouquet. No matter how businesslike their arrangement, it was still a wedding, and most likely the only one she'd ever have.

Alex disappeared into his study, closing the door behind him with a final click. So much for their celebrations. Anna gave her a sympathetic look, which only made her feel guilty.

'I think I should change,' she said as brightly as she could. 'And then we'll have something to eat.'

'But you've barely worn your wedding dress,' Anna protested. 'And you can't be acting as housekeeper on your wedding day of all days.'

'And who else will?' Milly answered with an attempt at a laugh. This felt like the least celebratory wedding day ever.

'I will,' Anna returned with spirit. 'You can't cook and clean today, Milly. I told you, we're having a celebration.'

'Anna, it's really not that kind of marriage,' Milly protested. 'Not yet,' she added, hating herself for continuing with the lie that she was madly in love with her boss—*and now her husband*. A tremor ran through her at the thought. What if Alex found out about the tale she'd been spinning? What if he believed it, and was horrified?

Anna's lower lip jutted out as she folded her arms. 'And what about tonight, Milly? Your honeymoon—'

'Anna.' Milly couldn't keep from blushing. The last thing she wanted to do was talk about *that* with her sister, or with anyone. She couldn't even *think* about tonight. Not yet.

'I'm *fourteen*, Milly,' Anna chided. 'And you're married. It needs to be special.'

'I really don't want to talk about this—'

'Fine. We won't.' Anna shooed her away. 'Go get changed. I'll take care of everything.'

'What?' Milly practically spluttered. She could not begin to imagine what Anna was thinking of doing, or what Alex's reaction would be. 'Anna, seriously, let's just relax, okay? There really doesn't need to be any fuss. Alex won't want there to be…'

'Don't worry,' Anna answered, half pushing her towards the stairs. 'You won't have to do a thing. I've got it all under control.'

Which worried her all the more. With mounting unease, Milly went upstairs to change. She took off her wedding dress slowly, her eyes on her reflection, noting the sorrow that had crept into them, casting shadows.

For a brief, painful moment, she imagined how different this day might have been. They'd have returned to the villa for a party, food and wine, laughter and dancing out on the terrace, until the sun set over the sea and Alex took her by the hand and led her back to the house, up to the bedroom.

He'd turn to her, his bright blue eyes turning sleepy and hooded as he tugged the zip down the back of her dress and the silky material fell away. Then he'd reach for her, and his lips would brush hers…

Goodness. Milly let out a shuddering breath as the effects of that image trickled through her like heated honey, making something both lazy and urgent unfurl deep inside. Such a different scenario had been all too easy to imagine, and yet she knew, she absolutely knew, it wasn't going to happen like that. She didn't even want it to happen like that. She'd told Alex the truth when she'd said she was wary of romance, cynical of love. Now that she was married, she most certainly could not go building castles in the air.

With a sigh, she turned away from her reflection, trying to banish the last remnants of that warm, sensuous feeling, and finished getting dressed. She needed to get back downstairs before her sister started festooning the villa with paper hearts and hiring someone to play the violin. Milly wouldn't put anything past her at this stage.

When Milly came downstairs, she saw that Anna had been busy getting things ready, although thankfully without any cringeworthy decorations or serenading violins. A table for two was set outside on the terrace, with the finest linens and crystal from the villa's cupboards. Yiannis must have been in on the plan because there was fresh food that had been brought from Halki—a mouth-watering Greek salad, crispy souvlaki and fresh pitta bread with several yogurt-based dips. Milly gazed at it in a mix of hope and apprehension; would Alex object to them sharing a meal together? She had no idea.

'This looks amazing,' she told Anna, grateful at least that her sister had only planned a meal, and not something more obviously romantic. 'But you should join us, Anna, and Yiannis, too. It is a celebration, after all—'

'Absolutely not,' Anna returned firmly. 'This is for the two of you. You need to get to know each other,' she added meaningfully, and Milly briefly closed her eyes. Alex would eventually twig to Anna's obvious attempts at creating romance, and then what would she say? He would no doubt be coldly scornful of such attempts, and Milly didn't think she could bear his contempt.

Yes, Anna was being young and sentimental, but she was a teenager and she'd had so little love in her life. Milly couldn't bear not to go along with it, even if the thought of Alex's reaction made her stomach cramp.

Anna ran to fetch Alex, and he strolled out onto the terrace with a bland look on his face, taking the table for two in his stride, although he didn't look particularly pleased about it. Anna had, of course, disappeared.

'I'm sorry about my sister,' Milly began awkwardly when they were both seated. 'She means well, really…'

'At least she's pleased,' he replied shortly.

'Yes…'

'She reminds me of my sister, how she used to be,' Alex said, then looked away, clearly wishing he hadn't shared so much.

'Your sister?' Milly searched his face, startled by this admission, just about the last thing she'd expected in this moment. 'I thought you only had your stepbrother, Ezio.'

Alex's mouth compressed. 'I do. Daphne died some time ago.' He began to dish out some salad on both of their plates, clearly unwilling to say anything more on that painful subject.

'I'm sorry,' Milly said quietly. 'That must have been very hard.'

'It was.' The two words were clipped, a hint of a warning in them. *Don't push it, Milly*, she told herself. At least Alex had offered something personal, even if he hadn't quite meant to. The door had cracked open just a little, and every so often she would push it a little further open. With time and patience, she might get to know him.

And is that all you want from your husband?

Milly chose not to pay attention to that mocking little voice. She wouldn't even know how to begin to answer that question.

Alex gazed out at the tranquil sea, the sun blazing down, and then turned back to the woman seated across from him. *His wife.* Milly had changed from her lovely wedding dress to a simple sundress in pale green, the skinny straps showing off her shoulders. She did have freckles there. Alex found his gaze skimming to them again and again, the dusting of gold urging him to press his lips to each one. Something, of course, he had no intention of actually doing. No doubt Milly would be horrified if he did.

It had been well-meaning of Anna to dress up their day a bit, although Alex could tell Milly was uncomfortable with it, something that irritated him even though he knew the reaction was unreasonable. Hell, he was uncomfortable, too. It was just a meal, but it wasn't what they'd agreed to. Nothing about this day felt the way he'd expected it to.

He'd viewed the ceremony as nothing more than a hurdle to get over, a hoop to jump through, and yet the words the priest had spoken had oddly moved him, as had the ancient rituals he and Milly had participated in— crowned with laurel, their eyes meeting over the common cup as they drank... He'd known marriage was binding, but he'd seen it as nothing more than a legal contract.

The ceremony in the tiny church had made him realise it was something sacred, and the thought humbled him. Scared him a little, too. What if he couldn't protect Milly? *What if he hurt her?*

'Alex?' Her voice, as well as the light touch of her fingers on his, startled him out of his dark thoughts. 'You suddenly started frowning rather ferociously.' Her lips trembled as she tried to smile. 'Is...is everything all right?'

'It's fine.' Alex forced a quick, tight smile to his lips, feeling his scar pull across his cheek, reminding him yet again of the limitations of their life together. The limitations Milly wanted as well as him. 'My mind was else-where. I'm sorry.'

'It's okay.' Her forehead was crinkled in concern, her gaze scanning his face. He looked away, angling his face so his scars were less visible. Even now, *especially* now, he didn't want her to see him like this.

'Well, I'm glad Anna isn't scaring you off,' Milly said with a light laugh. 'She's so excited about everything...and I think she's read too many romance novels.'

'She thinks our marriage is romantic?' Alex turned back to her, arching an eyebrow. 'Have you told her the truth?'

'Well...' He watched with dispassionate curiosity as Milly's face coloured. 'Sort of. She's...' She swallowed, and his gaze was drawn to the sinuous movement of her throat. 'She's hoping we fall desperately in love.'

He schooled his face into a bland expression even as her words blazed inside him, igniting what...? Hope? Horror? It was, of course, an impossibility. 'I hope you disabused her of that notion,' he remarked coolly.

'Of course I did.' The words came with such vehemence that Alex had to look away. He was an idiot to think for a moment that Milly might have been thinking or wanting something else—something he had no desire for, in any case.

'Right. That's settled, then.'

'Yes, I suppose it is.' Milly stared down at her plate, and Alex watched her, wondering what was going on in her head. Was she relieved? Or was she already regretting their impetuous marriage, realising the price she'd paid was too high? Tonight loomed in front of them, heavy with expectation.

He knew he shouldn't care about her feelings, and she certainly didn't care about his. And yet the ceremony circled in his head—the words of the priest, the common cup, their hands joined in a lover's knot of fingers. It had meant something, at least to him. Far more than he'd ever intended it to.

'All right, you two!' Anna called out gaily as she came out on the terrace, brandishing a platter that held what looked alarmingly like a traditional wedding cake.

'Anna...' Milly half rose from her chair, her flush starting all over again, her eyes wide with dismay. 'Where did you get that...?'

'Halki is amazingly well supplied,' Anna answered blithely. 'And Yiannis helped me. It's been such fun.' She placed the platter with the cake on the table between them with a flourish. 'It's traditional wedding cake, with honey, sesame seed, and quince.' She made a face and Milly managed a little laugh although she still looked uneasy. 'I'd rather have chocolate.'

'How on earth did you get a wedding cake on such short notice?' Milly said. She slid Alex an apologetic glance, which he ignored. A cake wasn't going to make a difference to anything.

'The bakery had one in the window,' Yiannis supplied. 'It seemed ordained.'

Ordained. Fated. Words of romance rather than business. Yiannis was as much of a sentimental fool as Anna, both of them wanting to turn today into a fairy tale. It wasn't going to happen. The only fairy tale in which Alex had a role was *Beauty and the Beast*, and with him it wouldn't have a happy ending.

Still, for the sake of form, he managed a small, tight smile. 'You are both too kind,' he said, and he gave Yiannis a repressive look over the top of Anna's head. *Enough.* His driver gave a short nod.

'Cut the cake,' Anna instructed. 'Both of you at the same time. For good luck.'

'Is that a thing?' Milly said, narrowing her eyes in suspicion, and Anna just shrugged, innocence personified.

'Fine.' Alex rose, reaching for the knife Anna had brought along with the cake. He glanced at Milly, and then motioned to the knife. Hesitantly she took it, and then he wrapped his hand around hers, just as he had when they'd walked into church.

Together they cut into the cake, the knife sinking through the soft icing and sponge underneath, her hand slight and warm under his. As soon as they'd finished, Anna and Yiannis both clapped, and Milly yanked her hand away, and Alex stepped back.

'I have work to do,' he announced, watching Anna's eyes round with dismay. His wife, he noticed, looked relieved. Without another word he strode from the terrace. Milly had a short reprieve, he acknowledged grimly; they still had their wedding night to get through.

CHAPTER EIGHT

NIGHT HAD FALLEN. Milly stared out at the darkening sky, her belly a flutter of nerves. After Alex had retreated to his study Anna had insisted Milly have an at-home spa day, running her a bubble bath and doing her nails.

Considering she'd just had a host of treatments two days ago in Athens, Milly had hardly seen the need, but she hadn't wanted to disappoint Anna. She loved being with her, and, in any case, she'd needed a distraction as the wedding night had loomed closer.

As the sun had begun to set, Anna had announced that she was staying the night with Yiannis and his wife in the village, making Milly protest.

'Anna, you don't...'

'It's your *wedding* night, Milly. The last thing you need is a little sister in your space.' Anna had made a face. 'And truthfully, I kind of don't want to be here, you know?'

'It's not...' Milly had decided not to finish that sentence, mostly because she hadn't known how, and Anna had patted her shoulder.

'I'll be fine. I've been having so much fun these last two days, Milly, you have no idea.' Tears had filled her eyes and she'd blinked them away as she'd offered her a heartbreaking smile. 'Honestly, I feel like I have a life suddenly, instead of hiding away, just waiting for things to happen.'

'I'm glad you're here, Anna.' Milly had pulled her sister into a tight hug. 'Really glad.'

Anna had hugged her back before easing away with a bright smile. 'But I'm not going to be here tonight. So have *fun*.'

Fun didn't seem the right word, Milly thought as she paced the living room alone, dressed in a simple navy shift dress, yet another one of her outfits from those brought to her at the hotel.

She felt as if she were crackling with nervous energy, about to combust. *Where was Alex?* She hadn't seen him in hours, and yet she had no idea what she would say when she did see him. What she would do. And more importantly, more alarmingly and, yes, excitingly, what *he* would do.

Her mind blanked every time she started to think about it, even as her nerve-endings became hyper-aware and her heart began to thud, and that molten-honey feeling trickled through her, igniting aches she'd never felt before.

'Good evening, Milly.'

She whirled around to see Alex standing in the doorway, dressed in a white button-down shirt open at the throat and dark trousers. His hair was spiky and damp from a recent shower, his lean jaw freshly shaven. As always he angled his face so she couldn't see his scarred side, but, regardless, he was devastatingly handsome, and she felt herself go weak at the knees, swaying a little at the sight of him.

'H-hello.' Her voice came out breathy with nerves and inside her black flats her toes curled. Scars or no, he was so beautiful, and she was so plain. Did he desire her at all? She could tell nothing from his carefully bland expression. 'Anna has gone with Yiannis and his wife for the night,' she blurted, willing herself not to flush. 'To give us some privacy.'

'So Yiannis told me. That was very considerate of them.'

'Have you known Yiannis long?'

'Since I was a child.'

'You have roots here,' Milly observed. 'Yiannis, the villagers…'

'Yes.' He glanced away. 'We came here, as a family, when I was young. Holidays every summer, some of the happiest memories I possess.'

'And the villa…?'

'I've had it for ten years. Now come.' He spoke flatly as he held out one hand and Milly stared at him, trying not to tremble. This step felt as momentous as the one she'd taken before, into the church. There would be no going back.

His eyebrow lifted as he remained with his hand outstretched. 'Are you scared?' he asked, a hint of gentleness in his voice.

'A little,' she confessed.

His mouth tightened and he nodded. 'I will do my best to make this as quick and painless as possible.'

Which made it sound as if she was about to endure some awful medical procedure, and she hardly wanted *that*. Everything inside Milly shook.

'That's kind of you,' she said, because she was overcome with nerves and she didn't know what to say. She could hardly ask him to make love to her, could she? To kiss and touch her like the hazy images that kept flitting through her head and making her dizzy with desire?

Just the thought of admitting how she felt, opening herself up to such vulnerability, made her tremble in a whole other way. She couldn't do that. Now, more than ever, was a time to protect herself.

Alex's mouth twisted, tightening his scar. 'It's the least I can do, Milly. I'm sorry...' He paused, then shook his head. 'Never mind. This is the way it is.' He reached for her hand, his fingers sliding over hers and then tightening imperceptibly, drawing her to him. Milly's heart thudded in her chest.

They hadn't even *kissed*. They'd barely touched. And yet very soon they would be committing the most intimate act a man and woman could together, an act that would unite them for ever. She was terrified, and yet within that fear was a lick of excitement, an ember of need waiting only to be fanned into flame, if Alex would just show her some modicum of tenderness, of desire...

She knew she was attracted to Alex on a basic, physical level. Her body responded to his; even the expensive, woodsy scent of him enflamed her senses, stoking that ember. Yet Alex seemed completely unaffected by her as he led her away from the living room, up the stairs, towards his bedroom, striding along like a man intent on getting the job done.

But why should he desire her? In her head she heard Philippe's mocking voice. *'How could I want someone like you?'* And she tried to drown it out. She didn't want to think about Philippe now of all moments.

Alex opened the door to his bedroom and then sucked in a surprised breath. 'What...?'

Milly peered inside, her eyes widening as she caught sight of the creamy candles flickering on various surfaces, a bottle of champagne chilling in a silver bucket by the bed.

'I'm so sorry,' she mumbled, heat flooding her face as she thought of how this would look to Alex. 'This is Anna's work. Obviously.'

'Obviously?' he queried sardonically, and her blush intensified.

'I wouldn't do something like this.' Heaven forbid he think she was trying to make the mood romantic.

'Of course you wouldn't.' She couldn't gauge his tone as he strode into the room and began to snuff out the candles with the tips of his fingers, causing a sizzling sound with each one.

'Can't...can't you leave at least one?'

'I prefer the dark.'

'Please...just one. I don't want to trip over my own feet.'

He hesitated, his fingers hovering over the last candle. The air was full of the scent of acrid smoke. 'Fine,' he said shortly, and turned away. The room was lost in shadow now, the single candle barely piercing the darkness, the shutters closed against the starlit sky.

Milly stared at him through the gloom, her heart still thumping. 'What now?'

'What now indeed?' He let out a hard little laugh. 'Why don't we have a glass of champagne?' Alex reached for the bottle and popped the cork with quick efficiency; there was, Milly thought, nothing remotely celebratory about the sound. He poured a flute full and thrust it to her. 'This will help.'

'Help?' She took the flute and sipped at the crisp bubbles. 'You make it sound like medicine.'

'An anaesthetic, perhaps,' he drawled before draining his own glass.

'For what? Some *procedure*?' Her voice trembled. 'Is that how you see this?' She gestured to the empty bed, neatly made up and heaped with pillows.

'Don't you?' Alex challenged, his eyes piercing through the darkness.

'I… I don't know,' she admitted. She felt bound by her own fear. She wasn't brave enough to admit she wanted more, that she *felt* something for him, not when he was seeming so forbidding. 'Surely it's meant to be somewhat pleasurable.' She let out an uncertain laugh. 'You know more than I would, Alex.'

'It's been a long time since I've had that kind of pleasurable experience,' he told her sardonically, then he sighed. 'I'm only trying to make this easier for you, Milly.' He nodded towards her glass. 'Drink up.'

She did, gulping the champagne far too fast

so her head started spinning even more. She'd never had much tolerance for alcohol, and she felt it now, her stomach seething both from the champagne and nerves. She watched, her eyes widening, as Alex began to unbutton his shirt.

'What…what are you doing?' she practically yelped.

'Undressing. The marital act requires a certain amount of disrobing.' His mouth twisted in something like a smile. 'Are you shocked?'

'Surprised,' she corrected, her gaze drawn to the sculpted muscles of his chest as he undid the buttons of his shirt with the same brisk efficiency with which he'd opened the champagne. He was beautifully proportioned, the candlelight burnishing his impressive physique in gold.

'Let's get this over with as quickly as possible, shall we?' he remarked. 'The sooner you become pregnant, the better it will be for both of us.'

She stared at him in dismay, her mind swirling from both his words and the champagne she'd just guzzled on an empty stomach. His hands went to his belt buckle and Milly couldn't keep from making a little sound of—

something. She didn't even know what she felt. Her body responded to his, but her mind and heart were both in active rebellion. This had to be the most unromantic wedding night she could have ever conceived of…and yet that was why she was here, wasn't it? To conceive.

Alex nodded to her simple navy-blue shift dress. 'Do you need help with the zip?'

'No.' The word came out more vehement than she intended. She'd known Alex was businesslike, even cold, but she realised now she'd still hoped for some tenderness on their wedding night, some tiny hint of romance or affection. Instead he seemed more clinical than ever.

She turned away from him, fumbling with the zip. Maybe he was right, and they should just get this over with. Clearly he didn't respond to her the way she did to him, and that should be no surprise. She was plain; she knew that. She'd always known that. If he desired her at all, he surely would have handled this whole evening differently.

And, oh, she wished he had. Tears sprang to her eyes and she blinked them back furiously. *You agreed to this*, she reminded herself silently. *None of this should come as a surprise. This was part of the bargain.*

The zip snagged halfway down her back and she nearly wrenched her arm trying to pull it down further, letting out a little cry of frustration and despair as it continued to stick.

'Here.' Suddenly Alex was next to her, moving swiftly in the dark. She felt the heat of his bare chest, the brush of his arm, and she sucked in a breath as he gently removed her hand from the zipper and then slowly pulled it down himself. She sucked in a hard breath, her whole body hyper-aware as his fingers traced her spine, his breath fanning her neck, the moment spinning into something both taut and tender.

Heat bloomed inside her, unfurling like a precious flower, seeking sunlight. She swayed and he rested his hands on her shoulders; for a heart-stopping second his lips skimmed the nape of her neck and Milly couldn't keep from making a little mewl of desire. He stilled and she started to lean into him, longing for him to slide his hands from her shoulders to—where? *Anywhere.* She just wanted to be touched.

'Milly...' His voice was an ache, and it made

unexpected tears sting her eyes. He pressed his lips against her neck again, this time in the curve of her shoulder, and she shuddered, arching her neck so he could have greater access.

For a second it seemed as if anything, everything were possible; as if a whole world of experience and emotion shimmered before them. His hands tightened on her shoulders and his lips moved on her skin. A shiver of longing rippled through her.

Then, all of a sudden, Alex lifted his head, dropped his hands, and stepped away. Milly half turned to him, conscious of her dress pooling about her waist, the longing that had rippled through her still licking at her senses.

'Alex...?'

'We should get this over with.' Alex walked towards the bed, slipping off his trousers while she watched uncertainly. Why had the mood changed, plunged suddenly from sweetness to sensibility, or something worse? Cold, clinical business. Again.

'Alex...' She stopped, because she had no idea what she would say. *'Please touch me?' 'Can't tonight be different?'* She couldn't make herself say the words. Despite the desire coursing through her, she still wasn't brave enough to risk what she felt.

'Come on,' he said, and nodded towards the bed.

Wordlessly Milly slipped out of her dress and underwear, not knowing what else to do, walked silently to the bed and lay down, longing only for him to touch her again the way he had before. Surely he would…? Why *wouldn't* he? She looked up at him appealingly, excitement stirring once more inside her just at the sight of him—his blazing blue eyes, his midnight-dark hair, his bronzed chest. She trembled with excitement as she licked her lips and whispered, 'I'm ready.'

Frustration bit deep as Alex stared at Milly lying on the bed like some virgin sacrifice, looking as if she had to brace herself for what lay ahead. She was actually *trembling*.

In any case, he supposed that was what she was—there could be no pretending she wanted to be here, that she was looking forward to being touched by him. She'd made her feelings plain enough, the way she'd gulped the champagne and insisted on unzipping her dress by herself.

For a moment, when he hadn't been able to resist touching her, he'd thought things might change. Then she'd shuddered and he'd realised what an utter fool he was making of himself. *And even if he wasn't*…even if she felt some small flicker of something…he couldn't risk it. He couldn't bear to be wrong. To be pitied… and by his wife.

Taking a short, sharp breath, his face angled away from her, he removed his boxers. Then he walked towards the bed and stretched out next to her, noticing the way she trembled even though he hadn't touched her yet.

She was tense as a bow, her toes pointed, her whole body rigid with expectation. Even so, she was lovely, her skin pale and golden, her body lithe and slender, her high, small breasts, small waist, and shapely legs all perfectly proportioned.

He ached to touch her, to explore every part of her body with his hands and mouth, and to have her do the same to him. Learning each other's bodies like living maps…but of course that was a nonsense. She didn't want to so much as *touch* him, much less explore.

Still Alex couldn't bring himself to climb on top of her like some rutting stag. Gently he placed his hand on her hip, her skin cool and silky beneath his palm. She let out a shuddering breath. He slid his hand from her hip to her breast, unable to keep himself from the caress, longing for more.

Her breast filled his palm perfectly and he ran his thumb over the taut peak. Another shuddering breath and she bit her lip. Shame roiled in his stomach; clearly this was no more than an endurance test.

Alex removed his hand, his body already pulsing with need. It had been a long time since he'd been with a woman, and he knew it wouldn't take much to put him over the edge. Perhaps the kindest thing for him to do was, as he'd said before, simply to get it over with.

He rolled on top of her, bracing himself above on his forearms. Her eyes were still closed, her teeth sunk so deep into her lower lip she'd drawn blood. Self-hatred burned white and hot inside him. Was this really what it had come to? A woman who couldn't even look at him, who was tensing herself for his touch? Why had he ever thought marriage could be a good idea? Could *work*?

Her eyes fluttered open, her dazed gaze fixed on his face. 'Aren't you going to…?' she began, and Alex, hating himself even more, gave a terse nod.

'Yes.' He positioned himself at her entrance, nudging her thighs apart with his knee but they were rigid and unmoving. 'Milly, you have to relax at least a little bit,' he gritted. 'Otherwise…'

'I'm sorry.' Her voice was small, making him ache in an entirely different and more painful way. 'I just…' She took a hitching breath, making his guilt pierce even more deeply. 'I thought…' She stopped, and then she spread her thighs, inhaling sharply as he began to move inside her.

'Did I hurt you?' he asked in a low voice. He had barely *begun*.

'Not…not exactly…' She put her hands on his shoulders, clasping him to her, and even though he knew she was just bracing herself, the touch reached deep inside him. He couldn't remember the last time a woman had touched him, skin on skin, an intimacy he'd forgotten existed. It enflamed him even more, even as the shame of how he must be hurting her bit deeply.

He gritted his teeth as he slid slowly inside her, inch by precious inch, filling her tight warmth, pleasure flooding his senses as he sheathed himself fully. Her fingernails dug into his shoulders, her eyes clenched shut once more, her body still so very tense.

'Milly, relax.'

'I'm trying,' she gasped out with a nervous laugh that almost, improbably, made him smile. 'This is…very strange.'

'I know.' It was strange for him too, in an entirely different way. In the past, when he'd been with a woman, he'd been focused on her pleasure. It had been a source of both honour and pride, and yet this…

This was the opposite. Yet he couldn't imagine it happening any differently. Slowly Alex began to move, sweat beading his brow as he sought to make her as comfortable as possible, even though everything in him ached to find a faster and deeper rhythm.

After a few seconds, she began to match

him, her hips moving jerkily. When Alex looked down at her, he saw how her face was screwed up, a drop of blood on her lip from where she'd bitten it. His vision was blurred at the edges, his mind dissolving as he came close to the peak.

'Alex…' Her voice was a plea, although for what he didn't know. Could it possibly be pleasure—could she be feeling even a little of what he was? At that thought, he came in an intoxicating rush, his body spending itself inside her, the pleasure crashing through him in intense waves.

They lay entangled for a few heart-thudding moments until Milly started to squirm beneath him.

'I'm sorry,' she said, her voice muffled. 'But I think I'm going to be sick.'

CHAPTER NINE

ALEX ROLLED OFF her in a lightning-quick movement and Milly scrambled off the bed and raced to the bathroom, barely managing to shut the door before she heaved into the toilet. She should not have drunk that champagne. She'd never had a head or, for that matter, a stomach for alcohol, and the tension of the last hour had made it worse.

She knelt by the toilet, her cheek resting on the rim, feeling more wretched than she'd ever thought it was possible to feel. She hadn't expected violins and roses as Anna had wanted, of course she hadn't. She considered herself a practical person. And yet that...*that*...

That had been her wedding night. She sat up slowly, her body aching in strange places. She hadn't expected to feel so *overwhelmed*. She understood why Alex had called it the marital act. It had certainly felt binding. But she'd wanted to be touched, and caressed, and kissed, and none of that had happened, except for a few exquisite moments at the beginning, moments that she now treasured because she feared they would be so rare. Why had Alex stopped? Should she have done something differently? Perhaps if she had, he would have kept on with the lovely kisses and caresses her heart and body both cried out for.

Instead, those tantalising flickers of pleasure she'd felt when Alex had touched her had never had the opportunity to fan into flame. She felt unsated, a restless ache at her centre that she knew only Alex could satisfy, and yet, despite those wonderful moments that had given her such hope as well as pleasure, it seemed as if he didn't want to. Didn't desire her, at least not enough to prolong what had happened between them. Should she really be surprised? He'd never indicated in any way that he responded to her physically, *little mouse* that she was.

Milly drew a ragged breath and then reached for the thick terrycloth robe hanging on the back of the bathroom door, grateful to swathe herself in its soft warmth. She dreaded leaving the bathroom and facing Alex again, but she knew she couldn't stay in here for ever.

She rinsed her mouth, combed her fingers through her hair, and gave her bleak reflection a wry look. Surely things could only get better. If they were able to get *worse*...but, no.

They'd talk, she decided. She'd tell him that she didn't care about romance, but the bedroom side of things could surely be better. What man wouldn't want to hear that?

One who doesn't desire you.

Flinching at the thought, she took a deep breath and then opened a door and stepped into the bedroom.

It was empty.

Milly gazed around the space, taking in the rumpled duvet, the single candle still burning. Alex was gone...and so were his clothes. Her stomach cramped at the thought. Was that *it*? She hadn't thought they were going to cuddle all night, of course, but...

She'd expected a little more than this. She had to keep giving herself reality checks, because, no matter what she told herself, she still came up against disappointment again and again. He didn't think of her with romance or even affection. He didn't desire her physically. When was she going to get it through her thick skull?

She sat on the edge of the bed, still unwilling to let go of the frail thread of hope. Perhaps he'd gone to get some food or drink, or... something. Surely he wouldn't just *disappear*.

Except he had. She waited for half an hour before she acknowledged he wasn't coming back. Feeling sick at heart, she ventured out of his bedroom. As she tiptoed down hallways and peeked in empty rooms, she realised he wasn't even in the villa. He hadn't just left the room, he'd left the whole house. Left *her*. Disconsolate, feeling more rejected than ever, Milly crept back to her own room and her own bed.

She woke some time after dawn, groggy from lack of sleep, her body still aching along with her heart. She hadn't heard Alex come back, and she had a leaden certainty weighing her down inside that he hadn't. She didn't know where he was, and he hadn't seen fit to tell her. Was that indicative of how their whole marriage was going to be?

By lunchtime Alex was still nowhere to be

seen. Yiannis drove Anna back home, and she came into the house on a wave of enthusiasm, her bright eyes and ready smile making Milly realise afresh how much her sister wanted a fairy tale. And why shouldn't she? She'd had precious little happiness in her life.

'So?' Anna asked as she came into the kitchen where Milly was making a salad for lunch. 'How was it?' She held up a hand, pretending to shudder. 'Please don't give me any details. I just mean…was it romantic?'

That would be a big fat no, Milly thought sourly. After being on her own all morning she was starting to feel angry as well as incredibly hurt. Couldn't Alex at least have *said* where he was? What if he was hurt or lost, and she didn't even know it? And yet she doubted he was.

'It was fine,' she said as diplomatically as she could. 'It's going to take time, Anna. It's not a rom-com, okay?'

'I know.' Anna looked indignant, but it didn't last long. 'Did you like the candles? And the champagne?'

Milly thought of Alex snuffing them out with brusque precision. 'Very nice touches,' she murmured. 'Thank you.'

Alex did not make an appearance for the rest of the day—or that night. After her initial hurt, Milly decided she was relieved. It was easier to spend time with Anna without worrying that Alex was going to come frowning in on them. And if she kept telling herself that, she thought wryly, she might even start to believe it.

Anna, fortunately, had bought Milly's excuse that Alex had pressing work to do, and she didn't nag too much about where he was. Like Milly, she was enjoying the sister time they so rarely had.

After dinner, they piled on the sofa together and watched a rom-com, a big bowl of popcorn on their laps. Milly couldn't remember the last time they'd done something like that together—it had to have been before their parents had got divorced, when Anna was only seven or eight. Having her sister snuggling against her once again was a balm to her bruised heart. *This* was why she'd married Alexandro Santos. Not for whatever did or didn't happen in their relationship—or in their bedroom.

Still, both she and Anna felt the gap when

the film had finished, and Anna was heading off to bed.

'Where's Alex?' she asked uncertainly as Milly took their dirty dishes to the kitchen.

'He's working,' she said as matter-of-factly as she could, trying to hide the hurt and confusion she felt. 'Don't worry, Anna. Remember he's mega-rich?' Milly tried for a smile. 'He's got to make that money, you know. He'll be back soon.'

But the words felt hollow as she headed up to her own bedroom, wondering where her husband was—and when he would come back.

She found out the next day, from Yiannis.

'Alex went to *Athens*?' Milly stared at him in disbelief as he stood in the kitchen doorway, looking resolute but also a bit shamefaced at the news he had to deliver. Anna was still asleep; Milly had arisen at the crack of dawn, too restless to stay in bed. 'But why?'

'Work.'

Work. Of course. Still, she felt numbed by the news. He hadn't even said goodbye. The last time she'd seen him she'd been racing from his bed, about to be sick. 'When will he be back?' she asked, trying to sound practical rather than devastated.

Yiannis gave her a sorrowful look. 'I don't know, Kyria Santos.'

Kyria Santos. The name jolted her. She was Alex's wife, and yet she didn't feel like it. She felt even *less* important than she had as his housekeeper, having been utterly dismissed and ignored after giving so much of herself to him.

'I'm sure he'll be back soon,' she said, trying to sound matter-of-fact, and feeling she'd failed. But surely he would return in a day or two? He still needed an heir, presumably. What happened to three times a week?

But the days passed and Alex didn't return. He didn't even ring, and when Anna asked her why she didn't call him, Milly was too ashamed to admit she didn't have his mobile number, and she was too proud to call his office like some cold-calling supplicant.

She tried to ignore the hurt that needled her at inopportune moments, the memory of his touch that had been so sweet, and then how awfully it had all ended. She wished she knew what was going on in his head, never mind his heart, but she felt as if she had no clue about him at all. He was as much a stranger as ever—even more so, because now she was married to him.

As the days passed Milly did her best to relax into time spent with her sister, whether it was curled up on the sofa watching films, or strolling along the beach, or having a coffee in the village. The time was precious and fleeting, for all too soon three weeks had passed and Anna needed to return home to get ready for school.

'I'm going to miss you so much,' Milly said, her voice choking as she watched Anna pack her bag. Yiannis had given her the message from Alex that Anna would return to Rome via his private jet, and Milly tried not to feel stung that he hadn't deigned to tell her himself.

'Perhaps I'll be able to visit for a weekend some time,' Anna suggested. 'Or for Christmas...'

But Christmas felt like an age away. 'I'll make sure of it,' Milly said firmly. She intended to use a chunk of her five million euros to give Carlos an incentive to let Anna consider Naxos her home. She was just working up the courage to confront him.

And what about Alex? More and more she felt the need to talk to him, to confront him about the nature of their marriage. It had been over two weeks since their wedding day, and she'd not had one word from him save for the message from Yiannis. It was more than an insult; it was cruel. She hadn't thought him capable of such unkindness, and the fact that he was unsettled her. What kind of man had she married after all?

'He'll come back, Milly,' Anna said softly, as if she could read her unhappy thoughts. Perhaps she could. 'I'm sure he will.'

'Yes, I know he will,' Milly returned with false cheer. She wasn't sure of any such thing, but she wasn't going to let her sister worry. 'Ring me as soon as you get back, all right? And I want to hear everything about your new school…'

'Of course.' Anna threw her arms around her and Milly held on tight. 'You'll get bored of me prattling on about it, I'm sure.'

'Never,' Milly returned. 'Never, ever.'

The house felt even emptier after Anna had

gone; Yiannis had driven her to the airstrip, with Milly accompanying, waving her off onto Alex's luxurious jet that she'd never even seen before. Back at the villa, Milly wandered around the empty rooms, battling a swamping sense of loneliness she'd never experienced before, at least not in the villa.

She loved it here. It was the first place she'd really been able to think of as home. And yet now the rooms held memories that taunted her at every turn. The study, where Alex had asked her to marry him. The pool area, where they'd spoken in the dark and she'd seen his scars. The bedroom, where she'd felt both the sweetest, briefest pleasure and the most heart-rending pain.

Where she'd once been cheerfully productive, tidying rooms, weeding the garden, shopping in the village, now she felt adrift, restless and bored. Waiting…and she had no idea how long she would have to wait for, or what would happen when Alex finally returned. *If* he would return.

His marriage was a mistake. Two and a half weeks had not shaken that certainty from his core. Every time he closed his eyes, Alex pictured Milly's terrified face, heard her whimpered words. *'I think I'm going to be sick.'*

What had he been thinking, believing he could marry a woman? That either of them could endure it? He'd left Naxos immediately; he knew Milly would be relieved and he hadn't been able to bear the thought of seeing the revulsion on her face yet another time.

No, better to stay away. And now it had been over two weeks, and any chance of a pregnancy—although Alex could hardly credit that such an awkward act could result in something so fortuitous—could be dismissed. All he had to do was call Milly and ask her. Assuming she wasn't pregnant, he would have the marriage annulled. His mistake would be rectified. They could both go on with their lives.

Autumn crisped the air, a few leaves fluttering down outside his office window, when Alex steeled himself to make the call. He listened to the house phone in Naxos ring, wondering if Milly would pick up. What had she been doing these last few weeks? Anna, he knew, had gone back to school. He'd made all the arrangements himself, and even now he allowed himself the barest flicker of pleasure that he might grant Milly some small happiness in that regard.

'Hello?' She sounded tired, he noted, and even dispirited.

'Milly, it's Alex.'

He heard her suck a breath in sharply. '*Now* you call.'

'It's been over two weeks.'

'So? Is that some deadline?' She let out a harsh laugh that sounded like despair. 'Where have you *been*, Alex?'

'Working.' He could feel himself prickle defensively; she sounded accusing but he'd been offering her a kindness.

'I know you've been working, but...why did you leave so suddenly? I came out of the bathroom...' She stopped, her voice choking before she drew a steadying breath. 'I thought you wanted an heir. You're not going about the most effective way to get one.'

'Are you pregnant?' he asked bluntly.

'*Pregnant?*' Another one of those awful laughs. 'Are you serious?'

'I know it is unlikely, but I need to ask. It's been two weeks, so I believe you could take a pregnancy test if necessary?' He'd looked it up online, but he was by no means an expert in these matters.

'No, I'm not pregnant,' she said after a moment, her voice sounding suffocated. 'I don't need to take a test.'

'Then we can have the marriage annulled.'

'What...?' Her breath came out in a rush. 'Why?'

'I realised it was a mistake,' Alex said flatly. 'And I'm sure you've come to the same conclusion.'

'But why?' She sounded bewildered rather than the relief he'd expected, and it unsettled him. This was really not the way he'd expected the conversation to go.

'I don't think we need to go into details, do we, Milly? Our wedding night spoke for itself.'

'About that—'

'I don't wish to discuss it. The pertinent facts remain unchanged. You may keep the five million euros. If you wish to remain as housekeeper, you may. Nothing need change for you.'

'Except, of course, the fact that I would no longer be married.'

'I hardly think that would bring you distress.'

'What is that supposed to mean?' Now she sounded angry, and he didn't understand it. He'd expected a sigh of relief, a stammered apology perhaps. Not this indignation, almost as if she were hurt. Or was it just her pride that was dented?

'Let's not quibble—' he began, only to be cut off.

'Quibble!'

'Regarding your sister, I've arranged for her to board at the music academy, so she does not need to reside with Carlos Bentano. Holidays she can spend with you.'

'What...?' Milly's breath came out in a sudden rush. 'How did you manage to arrange that?'

'Bentano is a reasonable man, when his comforts are put in jeopardy. His house is heavily mortgaged and he faces foreclosure. I had the mortgages transferred to me.'

'Alex, you didn't have to—'

'Anna is my family now,' he cut across her. 'Of course I will take care of her.'

'But she's not your family, if our marriage

is annulled,' Milly pointed out sharply. 'You have no responsibility for her then.'

Alex was silent, unsettled by her reasoning. He'd felt strongly about making sure Anna was provided and cared for. He'd failed his own sister, but he wouldn't fail Milly's. But of course she was right; once their marriage was annulled, he would have no relation to or responsibility for Anna. In all likelihood, he'd never see either Anna or Milly again. Why did that prospect give him a sudden, keen sense of loss, like a punch in the gut? He barely knew either of them.

'Even so,' he said. 'It is done.'

'Why are you doing this, Alex?' Milly asked softly. 'How can you be so kind and so cold at the same time? Can't we just...talk?'

'There's no point.'

'What about your heir? Your business?'

'It will go to Ezio eventually.' He hated the thought, but he would learn to live with it. 'I will put as many safeguards in place to keep him from running it into the ground.'

'I don't understand you,' she burst out. 'Why—?'

'I didn't ask you to,' he cut across her swiftly.

He didn't want to do a post-mortem on their failed marriage. It would serve no purpose, and every word, every memory, was agony.

'I know you didn't,' Milly said with quiet dignity. 'You've made that very, very clear.' And with that she hung up the phone, the slam of the receiver into the cradle blasting in Alex's ear.

He tossed his mobile on his desk, turning towards the window. She was angry, which he didn't entirely understand. He'd made the call expecting her to be relieved, bracing himself for the whoosh of breath she'd release, the burden lifted from her slight shoulders. Instead she'd sounded bewildered. Disappointed. Even hurt.

Or was he just projecting his own feelings onto her? Because the agony of their wedding night was a scar he'd have to bear, worse than any on his face. Her revulsion. Her fear. Her utter disgust…

He needed to stop thinking about it. His brief association with Milly James had opened up a part of himself he'd thought had been locked away for ever. She'd peeled back a protective layer without even trying to and he needed to find it again. Rebuild his defences, so no one could ever get close again. That, Alex knew, was the only way forward.

CHAPTER TEN

MILLY WALKED AROUND the villa in a daze of shock for two days, Alex's awful conversation running through her mind, before she galvanised herself into action. She couldn't leave it like that. She certainly couldn't let *him* leave like that, not least of all because Alex's brusque rejection of her reminded her too much of her past. Her entire childhood, and, really, her whole life, she'd been tidied out of the way when her parents couldn't be bothered to deal with her.

It reminded her of Philippe's cruel rejection as well, except Alex was so unlike Philippe. He was honest, or at least she'd believed him to be, and for that reason alone she needed to have a face-to-face conversation. She deserved one.

So, Milly decided, she was going to go to Athens and beard the lion in his twenty-second-floor den. She told Yiannis first, betting on the fact that Alex hadn't told anyone about the proposed annulment yet, and because she knew she needed his help to get there, just as she had before.

'I fancy a shopping trip to Athens,' she said as casually as she could one sunny morning in early September. 'Could you drive me to the ferry?'

Yiannis looked conflicted. 'Kyrie Santos won't like you taking the public ferry—'

'I took it before,' Milly objected. 'Thousands of people take it all the time.' And she was quite sure *Kyrie Santos* didn't care what she did, or how she did it.

Yiannis started to shake his head. 'Yes, but that was before you were married. Kyrie Santos is very protective of his own. If you wait a day or two, he can have the yacht back here—'

'But that would be such a waste,' Milly protested. 'And actually...' she lowered her voice conspiratorially '... I want to surprise Alex with my visit.' Which was true enough, if not in the way Yiannis might think or hope, judging by the light sparking in his eyes. She knew Yiannis and Marina, just like Anna, were desperate to see a happily-ever-after. And while

Milly had no illusion that *that* was going to happen, she still wanted answers, if nothing else.

Yiannis still looked torn. 'I don't know, Kyria—'

'Milly. You called me Milly before I was married. And you're not my keeper, Yiannis.' She gentled her words with a smile. 'I'm a grown woman, and I've lived on three different continents in my lifetime. I can do this. All I'm asking is for you to make it a little more convenient.'

He finally agreed, even giving her the key to Alex's flat, and Milly wasted no time in packing a bag. She still didn't really have a plan besides getting to Athens and confronting Alex, but that was enough to go on. She could think about it on the ferry, or make it up as she went along. The important thing was that she be able to see him face to face. If he'd even let her.

The trip across the Aegean was choppy this time of year, and Milly spent most of the six hours being sick over the railing, so by the time she arrived in Athens she was wrung out like a dish cloth. Not the most auspicious start to her visit, but she was still determined, at least.

Even though the key to Alex's flat felt as if it were burning a hole in her pocket, she chose instead to rent a room at a modest hotel, not wanting to run into him by accident when she was unprepared.

She showered and changed, regarding her rather wan appearance in the mirror with a wry grimace. She certainly did not look her best, but she doubted there was much point in making herself up anyway. It wasn't as if she was about to seduce him. He'd made his physical feelings for her very clear.

She had just stepped into Syntagma Square, where Alex had his offices, when she saw the flashing sign for a chemist's. She paused, because, despite having told Alex on the phone that she wasn't pregnant, she hadn't actually had a period since their wedding and she knew she probably should have. The irregularity was undoubtedly down to stress—what else could it be?—but just to be sure she went into the chemist's and, in halting Greek, asked for a pregnancy test. The chemist was all beaming smiles as he fetched her one, and Milly paid for it and shoved it to the bottom of her bag. She'd deal with that potential complication later. It was just a precaution, anyway. It seemed hard to believe that a single brief and loveless act could have resulted in a baby.

'Kyrie Santos is very busy,' the receptionist in the lobby of the gleaming skyscraper informed her repressively when Milly asked for him. It was a different woman from the one she'd dealt with before, when she'd said she was Alex's fiancée, and far snootier. 'And,' she added with something like relish, 'he never receives visitors.'

'He'll receive me,' Milly informed her shortly, although she wasn't at all sure. 'I'm his wife.'

The receptionist's mouth dropped open as she took in Milly's rather rumpled appearance with barely masked derision. 'His *wife*?'

'Yes, his wife. Now, why don't you ring him and tell him I'm here, before you embarrass yourself any further?' Milly had never talked to anyone like that in her life, and yet she couldn't deny it felt good. After a lifetime of being stepped on or pushed aside, she was finally sticking up for herself. Alex's rejection had pushed her into it, made her strong. She only hoped it did some good.

The receptionist picked up her phone, muttering into it in Greek, while Milly waited, trying to look calm and assured instead of terrified. After what felt like an endless moment, the woman put the phone down and nodded. 'You may go up.'

Her heart felt as if it were climbing into her throat as she soared upwards to the office that covered most of the twenty-second floor. What would Alex say when he saw her? What would *she* say? She hadn't thought this out carefully, simply running on pure adrenaline and emotion.

The doors pinged open and Alex stood there, glowering. 'What are you doing here?'

'Seeing my husband,' Milly fired back as she stepped out of the lift. 'Or was that not part of your *terms*?'

'The terms are moot,' Alex returned evenly. 'Considering our marriage is about to be annulled.'

'Yes, about that. Does annulment count the same as divorce?'

'What?' Alex looked nonplussed as Milly

strolled into his office, trying to hide how she trembled. Where had she got this courage? And what was she going to do with it? 'What does that matter?'

'Because the prenuptial contract stated that you owe me another five million euros if you divorce me.'

Alex closed the door behind him, looking incredulous. 'Is that why you came here? To demand more money?'

'No,' Milly cried with ragged emphasis. 'I came here for a straight answer, Alex. How do you think it feels, to have your husband walk out of your wedding night and then disappear for three *weeks*? And then the next communication is that he is intending to annul your marriage?' Tears started in her eyes but she blinked them back furiously, determined to stay strong. 'How could you be so cruel?'

'Cruel?' If anything her husband looked even more incredulous. 'I wasn't being cruel, Milly. I was being kind.'

She let out a harsh laugh, just as disbelieving as he was. 'Then you have a very twisted idea of kindness. Do you know how awful I felt? How…how rejected?' She sniffed, folding her arms and tilting her chin in a pointless effort to hide the worst of her pain.

Alex shook his head slowly. 'Milly, if anyone felt…rejected…' He took a swift breath. 'Look, there's no getting around the plain fact that our wedding night was a disaster. I tried to make it as—as endurable as possible, but I know you still found it difficult to…' He blew out a breath, colour slashing his cheekbones, his scars mottled red. 'To touch me. Or even look at me.'

Milly stared at him in confusion. 'What…?'

'Come now, Milly, let's not prevaricate. It was obvious.' He strode to his desk and sat behind it, as if he could turn their fraught conversation into a business meeting, as usual. 'I was trying to spare either of us any further discomfort. Marriage was a foolish choice for someone like me.'

Milly stepped closer to him, her mind racing with all he'd said—and hadn't said. Could this really be about his *scars*?

'Someone like you? Who is that, exactly?'

Impatiently Alex gestured to the scarred side of his face. 'Do I have to spell it out for you?'

'Yes, I actually think you do.'

His mouth compressed, his nostrils flaring. Milly forced herself to stare him down. 'I disgusted you, Milly. That much was clear. I disgusted you so much you were sick.' The words fell like lashes on her back, on her heart.

'Alex, I was sick because I'd guzzled too much champagne.'

'One glass—'

'On an empty stomach, and far too many nerves. I was terrified, Alex. I was a virgin.' Her voice wobbled. 'You knew that, didn't you?'

Colour slashed his high cheekbones. 'Yes—'

'And did you ever think that maybe that's why I was scared, not because of some scars on your face?' Fury boiled through her, surprising her with its force. 'Could you stop thinking about yourself for one moment to think about how *I* felt? A virgin who had barely been kissed, on her wedding night with a man who was practically a stranger—'

'A man who repulsed you—'

'Oh, stop talking like that! I don't care about your scars. And if you had bothered to pay attention, you would have realised I wasn't repulsed at all. I *desired* you, you...you ninny!'

* * *

Alex stared at her in disbelief. Why was she pursuing this complete fabrication? 'Your actions said otherwise, Milly.'

'You're not listening to me,' Milly snapped. 'I was a virgin. I was nervous. I drank too much champagne on an empty stomach. *You didn't even kiss me.*'

Her words fell like hammer blows, shattering his illusions, and yet he still couldn't believe it. 'You didn't want me to kiss you.'

'How on earth do you know that?' she demanded, looking entirely fed up. Still Alex couldn't let it go.

'Everything you said and did told me so. You didn't want help with your zip…'

'Because I was nervous and you seemed so cold—'

'And when I did help you, you shuddered—'

'With desire, not disgust. When you touched me… Alex, I wanted you to touch me more. I was desperate for it, but you stopped.' Milly tilted her chin, colour flaming her face. 'What is it going to take to make you believe me, Alex? Do you think this is easy? How much do I have to humiliate myself?'

'The humiliation was mine—'

'No. I desired you.' Her voice trembled. 'You're the one who—who seemed not to want me.'

His mouth fell open as he stared at her, utterly shocked by this admission. 'I think I gave evidence of my feelings, Milly,' he said evenly.

'You mean because you could—you could complete the act?' She shrugged scornfully, her chin tilted at a haughty angle, her face the colour of a tomato. 'Most men can do that, as far as I can tell. It doesn't...it doesn't actually mean anything.'

Alex turned away abruptly, rubbing his hands over his face. Was it possible that he'd got this so terribly wrong? Had he let his own fears and weaknesses distort his perception that much?

'Why do you think I wouldn't desire you?' he asked finally, his voice low, his back still to her. Milly didn't respond for a long moment, and when she did her voice was small, suffocated.

'Because...because I'm plain. I know that. I'm a...a little mouse.'

'A little mouse?' He whirled around, furious on her behalf. 'Did someone say that to you once?'

'Yes—a man. Philippe.' Her throat worked convulsively as she swallowed. 'I thought I loved him, but it was just a mirage. A fantasy.'

Jealousy boiled through him, surprising him with its force. 'And what happened?'

'He didn't feel the same way. Well.' She let out a sad little laugh, her shoulders hunched as her gaze slid away. 'The truth is, he was a cruel and dishonest man. Charming, but it was nothing more than a veneer, and, after living with my mother, I thought I would recognise that, but I didn't. I fell for his lines.'

Alex's fists clenched. He hated this man already. 'What happened between you?'

'Nothing, really.' Her lips trembled as she tried to smile. 'I made a fool of myself, basically, following him around, listening to his lies. He told me he'd fallen in love with me, but then I...' She paused, swallowing hard, and he realised how difficult this was for her.

He was both humbled and shamed to realise she had her own painful memories, her own insecurities. Of course she did. How could he

have been so selfish, so arrogant, as to think
he was the only one?

'You don't have to tell me, Milly.'

'No, I want to.' Her chin lifted another notch.
'Because then maybe you'll understand where
I'm coming from, for once.' *Ouch.* He waited
while she fought for her composure to continue. 'He was one of my mother's cronies,
from when she lived in Paris. The circuit of
impoverished aristocrats and D-list celebrities.
Really, a stellar group.'

'How did you meet him?'

'He sought me out, because he knew my
mother. That should have sent the warning
bells ringing, but he seemed so sincere, and I
wanted to believe him. No one had ever shown
that kind of interest in me before.'

'No one—'

'I'm plain, Alex. I know that.'

'You're not—'

'Anyway.' She shook her head, refusing to
believe him, just as he'd refused to believe her.
'We started dating. He told me he loved me.
He...' Her voice faltered. 'He wanted us to
spend the night together, at a hotel. All very
romantic, but I was hesitant. It felt too fast.'

'Tell me,' Alex said in a low, deadly voice, 'that he didn't hurt you.'

'No, not like that. Just my feelings. We were at a party and I'd gone to the ladies'. I wasn't very comfortable there—it was his crowd, not mine. Anyway, as I came back I overheard him talking to his friends.' She bit her lip, sinking her teeth into it just as she had on their wedding night, her face shadowed with remembered pain. 'They were joking, taking bets as to when he would—when he would deflower me. I stood there, hardly able to believe it, and then he joked about how he'd have to grin and bear it, because he found me so...' She stopped, and Alex took a step towards her.

'Milly, don't. The man sounds like an utter bastard.'

'Well, I'm sure you can imagine what he said. And then one of his friends saw me, and nudged him, and he turned around and laughed in my face. He didn't even try to deny it. He told me he'd been given a dare, to seduce the plainest girl he could find. That's when he said it—*"Do you honestly think I could fall for a little mouse like you?"*' She bowed her head. 'Look, I know he was a jerk. I realise in that moment he was trying to save face in front of his friends. I know his words aren't some gospel truth. I'm… I'm over that.'

'Are you?' Alex asked in a raw voice. She'd faced the kind of rejection he hadn't let himself face, because he'd hidden himself away. She was, he realised, far braver than he'd ever been.

'Yes,' Milly said firmly. She lifted her head to look at him, blinking back tears, her jaw set. *So brave.* 'Yes, I am. But perhaps now you understand, Alex, why I acted the way I did on our wedding night. I had painful memories, too.'

His jaw clenched with self-recrimination. 'I wish I'd known.'

'You never gave me the chance to tell you. And I admit, I didn't really want to lay myself bare like that.' Despite everything, she managed a wry smile. 'I was bare enough.'

'I'm sorry,' Alex managed, the words feeling both strange and sincere. 'I didn't realise that. I didn't…' He shook his head. 'I suppose I was only thinking about myself.' Even though he'd convinced himself he was thinking about her, being kind when in reality he'd just been protecting himself. Again.

'So here we are.' Milly flung her arms out. 'Two people who got it all badly wrong, because they were both so scared.'

He opened his mouth to deny it, but how could he? As much as it shamed him, he had been scared. Scared of being rejected. Of being hurt. And so he'd hurt her instead.

'I'm sorry,' he said again.

They stared at each other for a long moment, the air tautening between them. 'So now what?' Milly finally asked softly. 'Are you still determined to annul our marriage?'

'I thought I was doing you a kindness.'

'And I'm telling you now you aren't.'

He took a deep breath, forced himself to ask the question. 'Do you really want to be married to me, Milly? Anna can stay in school. You can keep the five million euros—'

'I honour my commitments, Alex. My *vows*.' Her voice shook. 'And the truth is, I don't want to be rejected again. I'm not looking for love, but I thought—I hoped—we could have some kind of affection between us. But perhaps now I need to ask you the same question—do you really want to be married to me? Do you—do you desire me?' Her voice trembled and broke on the words.

For a moment Alex couldn't speak. He couldn't believe she'd suffered from as much doubt as he had—*and he hadn't even realised.* And now she was asking him point-blank to admit the truth, and he knew he would, he had to, no matter what it cost him. Even if she turned away. 'Yes,' he said in a low voice. 'I do. Truly, I do. You're lovely, Milly. The freckles on your shoulders…'

She let out an incredulous laugh. 'Of all the things…the freckles on my *shoulders*?'

'I dreamed about kissing them,' he admitted, heat unfurling through his body at the thought. He wanted to kiss them now. 'Kissing all of you…'

Her eyes smoked and blazed as she met his gaze boldly. 'Then do it,' she said.

CHAPTER ELEVEN

HEAT BLOOMED AND rushed through Milly as she stared at Alex, daring him to prove his desire. Needing him to desperately, because if he didn't do something, she would. Or else she would combust.

'You mean...' he began, looking startled, and she wondered how such a powerful and beautiful man could have become so uncertain. The scars were deeper than they looked.

'Yes. Now.' Her voice turned ragged with her need. 'Please.'

He took a step towards her, and then another. Milly held her breath. Then he was standing in front of her, looking at her in wonder. 'Are you sure...?'

'How many times do I have to say it?' Milly demanded.

Gently he touched his fingers to her lips, and even that sent need arrowing to her core.

'I haven't kissed a woman since before the accident. I haven't so much as *touched*...'

'Touch me.'

And then he did. He bent his head, one hand anchored to her waist as his lips skimmed hers. Her mouth opened hungrily, already wanting more. She reached up and put her hands on his strong shoulders, drawing herself to him. As their bodies collided she sucked in a hard breath. Everything in her felt as if it were on fire.

And amazingly, wonderfully, Alex seemed to feel the same, for his brush of a kiss turned into something hungry and demanding, something wonderful. His mouth plundered hers as he pulled her tight against him.

'Now do you doubt me?' he demanded in a growl against her mouth, and she let out an incredulous laugh, intoxicated by the need she felt in both him and herself.

'Show me more.'

And he did, hoisting her by the hips and seating her on his desk as he swept papers away with one commanding hand. He parted her thighs, standing between them, as he kissed her with both thoroughness and urgency. She drove her hands through his hair, careful even now to avoid his scars, unsure if they might pain him. Not wanting anything to break this moment.

'Touch me, Alex,' she half whimpered. 'Touch me more, *please*.'

He slid his hand along her thigh, making her squirm as his fingers found her bare flesh. And then higher still, and she let out a moan of both pleasure and frustration. *More.* She still wanted more.

And then he was at her centre, touching her with such intimacy and expertise that she felt as if she were flying apart. Still it wasn't enough.

Emboldened by her desire, she reached for his zip. Alex tore his mouth from hers. 'Milly…'

'You don't receive visitors, remember?' she said, feeling reckless, and his little smile made her want to sing.

Then his face darkened with passion as he tugged at his zip and pulled her even closer, settling himself between her thighs.

Milly braced herself against him as he began to slide inside her, the invasion both sweet and strange and *so much*.

'Tell me if I'm hurting you,' he gasped, and she shook her head, her head pressed against his shoulder as her body adjusted and together they found their rhythm.

'You're not. You're not at all.'

And then she lost the power to speak, to think; all she could do was feel the exquisite pleasure of his body inside hers, the overwhelming intimacy of it, this act that would bind them together for ever. Nothing could split this asunder. *Nothing.*

And when she came, it was like the splintering of stars, the word dissolving and then coming together again with a new, crystalline brightness as he cradled her in his arms, holding her as if he'd never let her go. And in that moment, she knew she didn't want him to.

Yet he did, easing back slowly, looking stunned by their explosive interaction. 'Did I hurt you?' he asked in a low voice, and Milly nearly laughed aloud.

'No.' She regarded him closely, trying to figure out what was going on behind those shadowed eyes. 'Did you think you did?'

'I lost control.'

'So did I.' She paused, the confidence that

their lovemaking had given her starting to seep away. She was cold and sticky and her skirt was rucked up to her hips. She wriggled to try to get it down and give herself a modicum of modesty. 'Does that have to be a bad thing?' she asked cautiously.

'No, I…' Alex shook his head, raking his hand through his hair as he turned away to do up his trousers. 'I never expected this.'

He didn't sound particularly pleased, and Milly had no idea why. Surely a physical attraction between them was a good thing, especially if he wanted a child? Briefly she thought of the pregnancy test in her bag, and then pushed the image away. She couldn't be pregnant. She couldn't deal with being pregnant, not now, so soon. Surely it had just been stress.

'Expected what, exactly?' she asked as she eased herself off his desk and straightened her skirt. Her lips felt swollen from his kisses, her body aching in a rather lovely way. Still, she felt the need for caution; Alex certainly seemed guarded. No matter how uninhibited they had been moments before, in the throes of passion, things clearly were different now.

'Expected us to have…a physical attraction.' He turned back to her. 'It wasn't in my planning.'

'Well, surely you can make room for it?' Milly suggested, trying to smile. 'It will make trying for a baby more pleasant, at least.'

'Yes, I suppose.' He still didn't look happy about it, though, and Milly wasn't brave enough any more to try to tease him out of it. In truth she had no idea what to do now.

'So you're not going to annul the marriage,' she said at last, because that felt like the most important thing.

Alex hesitated, making her freeze. Surely after what they'd just experienced, what they'd shared, he wouldn't…?

'No,' he said at last, sounding reluctant. 'I won't.'

Alex had no idea how to feel. What had just happened…what he'd just felt…what *Milly* had felt…

It had blown his mind. Destroyed all his preconceptions. And left him spinning in a void of unknowing, because nothing about their business arrangement had made him expect *that*.

And *that* had been amazing. Incredible. The best sex he'd ever had, because it hadn't just been sex.

And therein lay the problem. They were treading on thin ice, moving into dangerous waters. Emotional ones.

'Alex?' Milly straightened her skirt, looking uncertain. 'Why do you look as if you're not happy about this?'

'It's fine,' he said, which was no real answer at all. 'I just didn't expect…' he shook his head '…any of this.'

'Right.' She smiled shyly. 'Can't we just… consider this a bonus?'

A bonus. He stared at her as if seeing her for the first time. Her hair was tumbled about her shoulders, her face still rosy, her lips still swollen from his kisses. Looking at her now, he wanted her all over again, with a deep and abiding need that shocked him.

Of course Milly didn't know, and he wasn't about to tell her, that he hadn't physically desired a woman like this in nearly two years. He hadn't desired a woman at *all* in that time; he'd never thought to feel that need again—and now it was overpowering him. It was thrilling, but it was also alarming. It made him vulnerable. It made him weak.

'Alex...?'

He retrained his distant gaze on her. He was being irrational. *Emotional*, which was something he tried never to be, because he knew where it led. A physical relationship didn't have to mean anything. It hadn't before. Yes, they were married now, and *that* meant something, but this didn't have to. This could be just what Milly had said...a bonus. A very nice bonus.

'Sorry.' He gave her a quick smile. 'I like your thinking.'

Her face lit up as she smiled shyly. 'You do?'

'Yes, I most certainly do. It's just taken me a little while to catch up.' She scanned his face, waiting for more. Alex reached for her and she came willingly into his arms, something else that felt strange. He could get used to this, he realised, and then where would he be?

'This is an unexpected perk,' he murmured, and then brushed a kiss across her lips. She responded instantly, fitting her body to his, wrapping her arms around his neck, tempting him to take it further. A lot further.

But now was neither the time nor the place, despite what had just happened right on his desk. He needed to regroup, regain control, and figure out exactly how he was going to handle this unforeseen complication. *This bonus.*

'Why don't you go back to my flat?' he suggested. 'Make yourself comfortable, order in food. I'll join you as soon as I've finished up here.' He turned to reach for his phone. 'The doorman will give you the key. I'll call a limo...'

'I already have a key,' Milly confessed. 'Yiannis gave it to me when I told him I was coming to Athens.'

'He did?'

'I told him I was coming to surprise you. I made it sound like...well, exactly like it happened, as it turns out.' Laughter bubbled up inside her and spilled out. 'I just didn't realise that was going to be the case.'

She sounded so happy, and Alex could hardly credit he had made her that way. And yet it made him wary too, because what happened when he inevitably disappointed or hurt her? When she found out the truth?

'That's easily dealt with, then,' he said with a smile. 'I won't even have to ring the doorman.'

'All right.' She hesitated, and he simply stood there, hands in his pockets, waiting for her to go. Half of him wanted to snatch her up in his arms and bury his head in her hair, bury himself inside her again and again and again. Because he could. Because she wanted him to. Because he'd never, ever expected this much and it scared the hell out of him.

'I'll see you soon?' she asked, a gentle query, and he nodded.

'Yes. Soon.'

'All right,' she said again, and then she was gone, the door clicking shut softly behind her, the only thing remaining of her presence the faint lemony scent of her perfume—and the detritus of his papers scattered on the floor from when he'd swept them away in a moment of pure, blazing passion.

What was happening to him? What had happened to *them*? Alex walked slowly to his desk and sank into the chair, still dazed by the whole surreal encounter. Less than an hour ago he'd been intending to annul the marriage.

He'd already called his lawyer to draw up the documents. And now…and now…

And now his marriage was going to look very different. Feel very different.

But not that different.

Alex let out a shuddering breath and reached for his papers. He still had work to do, a property deal in Sicily to look over, but he felt as if he couldn't concentrate on anything. His mind kept going back to the moments he'd had with Milly, when she'd stared him straight in the face and said, *'I desired you.'* When she'd thrown back her head, her voice a throaty growl as she'd pleaded with him. *'Touch me, Alex. Touch me more, please.'*

He rose abruptly, his blood heated simply from the memories. He was half inclined to take off after her now, spend the rest of the day and the whole night in bed.

But, no. He needed to think. He needed to remember to stay in control, because Milly might have, incredibly, accepted the scars on his face, but she had no idea about the ones on his soul. She had no idea what he was capable of, how he'd failed the people he'd loved. And if she learned any of that, she wouldn't be able to look him in the eye. She wouldn't be able to stand being touched by him. He was sure of it, and he knew already it would hurt more because of what they'd shared.

He had to find a way to keep his distance... and enjoy this *bonus*.

Which, Alex acknowledged, he should be able to do without a problem. He was a man, after all, a man who had once had an active sex life, who had managed to separate sex and love with absolute ease. This shouldn't be a problem, he told himself grimly. He would make sure it wasn't.

CHAPTER TWELVE

MILLY STEPPED INTO Alex's penthouse apartment in one of Athens' best neighbourhoods with a rush of released breath. Her body still tingled from their lovemaking, her mind still reeled. So much had happened. So much had changed. She hoped.

She put her bag down by the door as she took in her minimalistic but clearly luxurious surroundings. The penthouse was open-plan, with a soaring glass ceiling and floor-to-ceiling views of the Acropolis. White and grey leather sofas were scattered over the gleaming black marble floor, and a huge canvas of white with a few artful black splotches and lines took pride of place over the fireplace.

Milly stepped closer and realised the painting wasn't the stereotypical abstract modern art; it was a child's drawing that had been magnified, stick figures with lopsided heads and wide smiles. Her heart constricted. Why would Alex have such a picture in his flat? What did it mean to him?

She studied it for a few more minutes noting there were three people in the picture, two adults and a child. Who had drawn it? Or did it mean nothing—it was some interior designer's attempt at modern art?

She turned away to explore the rest of Alex's domain: a large kitchen of gleaming chrome and granite led off the main living area, and down a corridor were two sumptuous bedrooms, one done in navy, one done in cream, each with its own luxurious bathroom. Spiral stairs at the end of the corridor led up to a private gym and a study, as well as an enormous roof terrace with an outdoor pool, the water sparkling under the midday sun.

It was every bit as luxurious as the villa on Naxos, and yet besides the child's drawing over the fireplace, it felt strangely impersonal. Just like the villa, there were no photographs, no knick-knacks, no books or mementoes. It was a blank canvas, a clean slate, almost as if Alex had tidied away evidence of himself on purpose.

Back downstairs, Milly wondered what would

happen when Alex returned home. She recalled his remoteness with a prickle of unease; no matter how explosive their lovemaking had been, he'd still kept a certain emotional distance that she supposed was second nature to him. He was a guarded, private man, and his scars had made him even more so.

Which she'd known going into this marriage, and still had to accept now. The trouble was, Milly acknowledged, what had happened between them today had changed things for her. She knew it wasn't supposed to, and sex was meant to be just sex, but it hadn't felt like that at all. It had felt intimate. Incredible. *Important.* And she was going to have to keep reminding herself that Alex definitely did not feel the same way…which was a good thing, because, no matter what their physical chemistry was like, Alex Santos was not a man to give your heart away to. He certainly didn't want to take it, and she didn't want to be hurt. Again. Keeping things on a physical-only level was better for both of them.

With hours before Alex was due to return, Milly decided to take advantage of the decadent bathroom, and filled the sunken marble tub right to the brim with hot water and plenty of luxury bubble bath. As she reached for a fresh change of clothes from her bag, her hand closed around the slim cardboard box she'd bought this morning. The pregnancy test.

For a second she hesitated; now would be a perfect time to take the test, to make sure she wasn't pregnant. But without fully thinking about what she was doing, Milly shoved the box deeper into her bag. She was almost sure her missed period was down to nothing more than stress…there was no need to take the test right now. She could wait a little while.

But as she sank into the heavenly hot and fragrant water, Milly had to acknowledge her reluctance to take the test was more than the prospect of wasting it. She didn't want to be pregnant yet. She didn't want to upend things, not when she and Alex were starting to get to know each other. When their marriage could be just a little bit more than the business arrangement they'd both agreed on. She could wait a few days, or even a few weeks. In all likelihood her period would arrive by then anyway.

As evening approached, nerves started to

flutter in Milly's belly, of both trepidation and excitement. Since there was no food in the house, she ordered a meal to be delivered, and then she spent an age redoing her make-up before wiping it all off. This was ridiculous. It was too late to try to impress Alex, and yet she wanted to do something to show things had changed between them.

When the door to the flat finally opened, she was speechless with nerves, only able to stare at him across the darkened room, moonlight spilling in through the windows. Alex stood still for a moment, framed by the light from the hallway, the electric blaze of his blue eyes visible even in the dim lighting, and sending spirals of excitement and desire coursing through Milly. All she could do was stare—and want.

Alex's briefcase fell from his hand with a *thunk*. In one fluid movement he closed the door behind him.

'I've been waiting for you,' Milly said breathlessly, half wondering if Alex felt the same taut need that she felt, running through her like a wire, pulling her to him.

Except she wasn't being pulled; he was coming towards her, shedding his jacket and tie as he walked. Her breath bottled in her chest, her heart thumping double time as Alex discarded his tie and then pulled her into his arms. His mouth came down on hers and that was all she needed for the excitement to burst out of her in a frenzy of response; she kissed him back with all the urgency and passion she felt, her hands clawing at his shirt, longing to feel his bare skin on hers.

Shedding clothes, they tripped and stumbled their way towards the bedroom, and then fell on the bed in a tangle of limbs. Milly gasped and arched as Alex's mouth roved over her, branding her skin with his hot touch. She came alive under his hands in a way she'd never experienced, never expected, and when he finally began to move inside her she cried out in both pleasure and surprise, that again it could be so incredible between them. So important.

They were lying on the twisted sheets, their hearts both still thudding, neither of them having said a word, when the doorbell rang. Alex tensed and Milly laid her palm flat on his chest, revelling in the feel of him.

'That will be the food I ordered,' she said.

'Ah.' Alex relaxed, a smile teasing his mouth.

'I'll get it,' she said, and she rose from the bed, flinging on a dressing gown before hurrying to the door.

As she signed for the food and took the order, her body feeling sated and sleepy and yet also achingly alive, she realised she was buzzing in places she didn't even know she had. She was also happier than she'd been in a long while.

This was definitely some bonus, she thought, a smile curving her lips as she returned to the bedroom with several containers of takeaway.

'Why do you look like the cat who got the cream?' Alex asked, stretching in bed, his voice holding a teasing note that was entirely new—and wonderful.

'I did get the cream,' she dared to tease, and he laughed, another sound that was both strange and wonderful. She felt as if she were chipping away at Alex's icy exterior, and the glimpses of both the heat and heart underneath thrilled her.

She shed her dressing gown and got back in bed, and together they relaxed, eating Chinese food amidst the tangle of the duvet. Milly felt buoyant with happiness, as if she could float right up to the ceiling.

'So did you close any property deals today?' she asked, and Alex looked surprised by the question.

'Do you really want to know?'

'Of course I do.'

He shrugged. 'I'm working on a low-income housing development in Piraeus. It's an area of the country that has suffered from the economic crisis, and the housing stock is shockingly substandard in places.'

'That sounds like a worthwhile project.' For some reason Milly had imagined that Alex's property deals were for top-end resorts and hotels, not housing for people in need. 'Do you make money from that?' she asked curiously.

'Yes, assuming you do the thing properly. The houses are environmentally friendly and made of locally sourced building materials, and everyone employed to work on the project will be local. It's meant to revitalise the community, not just provide housing.'

'That's amazing, Alex.'

He shook his head. 'Not really, it's smart. There is a profit in it for me.' He looked at her seriously, the light-hearted expression dropping from his face. 'Don't start seeing me as some white knight, Milly, just because we're good together in bed.'

She felt her face warm because that was exactly what she'd been doing. Every little thing he did or said that was kind or good helped her construct a picture of him—the picture she realised she was desperate to see.

'I wouldn't say white knight exactly,' she said as lightly as she could. 'But why dismiss it when it's clearly something good?'

'I'm not dismissing it,' Alex said shortly. 'I'm just warning you.'

Stung now, she stared down at her half-eaten noodles. 'Of what, exactly?'

He touched her chin with his fingers, tilting it so she had no choice but to gaze up at him—his smile strangely compassionate. 'What we have is good, Milly. It's a bonus, like you said. An amazing bonus. But that's all it is.'

'I know that.' She spoke stiffly, embarrassed that he felt the need to give her such a warning. He could see right through her, and she felt as if she couldn't see him at all.

'I just don't want to disappoint you.'

'You won't, Alex.' She eased back so his hand fell away from her face. 'I'm going into this with my eyes wide open, trust me. I won't let myself be disappointed.'

He certainly knew how to ruin a mood. Alex watched Milly broodingly, half wishing he hadn't issued such a bleak warning, yet knowing he'd had to. He'd seen the stars forming in her eyes, and he even understood why. Their incredible physical intimacy made her want a deeper, emotional one. It was natural, expected. They both needed to guard against it.

The smart thing, he knew, would be to send her back to Naxos and get on with his work. Yet despite the words he'd just spoken, he was reluctant to do just that. They were married; they enjoyed each other's bodies. This could be simple.

'Why don't you stay in Athens for a few days?' he suggested. 'You could do some shopping, if you like.'

Milly wrinkled her nose. 'I've done enough shopping, thanks to the assistants you had come to the hotel before. But I would like to take in some of the sights. I've never seen the Acropolis, or any of the museums.'

'Then you must do so.' He gave her a wolfish smile. 'Tour Athens by day, and then we can entertain ourselves at night.'

She smiled back, but he saw the remnants of shadows in her eyes, and he knew she took his words as he meant them—another warning as well as a promise.

The next few days were some of the most pleasant Alex had ever known—and not just pleasant, but truly happy. He thought back to when Milly had asked him if he was happy, if he would be happy, and he'd told her being happy with their business arrangement was enough. But now that didn't feel like nearly enough, and he was far happier than he'd ever expected or hoped to be. It made him feel uneasy, because he knew all too well how happiness could be taken away. How he could destroy it.

But he pushed those thoughts away, determined to enjoy this brief respite. In a few days Milly would go back to Naxos; this was a moment in time, nothing more. They could both afford to enjoy each other.

And they did…both in bed and out of it. Alex was surprised at how much he enjoyed the out of it part, because when they were in bed, everything was explosive. But out of it, he found he liked chatting over a meal, or watching something inane on TV. He especially liked coming back to a warm and lit flat, to a *home*. As the days progressed, Milly filled the kitchen with food and started preparing their evening meals. Alex had told her they could order in, but she was insistent, saying how she liked to cook.

And he liked her cooking—liked the fragrant smells that filled the rooms, the simple but delicious meals they ate together. It felt like a family.

Which reminded him of their true purpose. 'Do you think you might be pregnant?' he asked matter-of-factly one evening as they lay amidst the tangle of his sheets, their hearts still thudding from the intensity of their lovemaking.

'Pregnant?' She tensed, and he didn't miss the flash of something that looked almost like fear streak across her face before she schooled her expression into something far more innocuous. 'It's a bit early, don't you think?'

'You're young and healthy, and the doctor said there were no medical issues.'

'Yes, but we've only been married a month, and we've been apart for most of that.' She let out a little, uncertain laugh. 'We don't have to rush things, do we?'

'Rush things?' He stared at her, trying to discern what was clearly making her uneasy. 'It's not a matter of rushing things. Nature will take its course, and we're certainly doing as much as we can in that regard.'

'Yes...' She looked relieved, and unease trailed along his spine. Was she hiding something—some fear, some feeling? What was she not telling him?

'I just wondered. You will tell me, of course, if you think you might be?'

'Of course.' She spoke quickly. 'Of course I'll tell you.'

Alex told himself to banish that faint unease as the days moved on, and it was easy enough to do so. And somehow the few days in Athens turned into weeks, and neither of them spoke about her going back to Naxos.

And then one day, when he came home from

work, the flat as lovely and welcoming as ever, she sprang something on him.

'Anna rang.'

'Oh?' As usual Alex dropped his briefcase and shed his jacket and tie. 'How are things at school?'

'They're really good.' She sounded hesitant, which made him wonder.

'And?'

'And she's been selected to play at a charity gala next week, a black-tie event. It's a huge honour, and she asked if we could go.'

'To Rome?'

'Yes.'

He stared at her for a moment, registering the nervous, beseeching look in her eyes. 'That's not a problem. You're not a prisoner, Milly. You're free to go. I have a suite on standby at the Hotel de Russie.' One he had not needed to use since his accident, but still. 'I'll make arrangements for you to stay there.'

'I don't want to go alone.' She spoke softly, imploringly, her eyes huge. Alex stilled.

'What are you saying?'

'Why don't you go with me? Anna asked

specifically for us both to go. She wants us both there.'

'At a charity gala? With hundreds of people present?'

Milly tilted her chin, a gesture Alex recognised for when she was settling in for a fight. 'Yes.'

'Milly...' He blew out a breath, resenting that she'd put him in this position. 'Do I really have to explain...?'

'I know you don't like to go out in public, Alex, because of your scars.' Milly spoke softly, but with determination. 'I understand that.'

'Do you?' he burst out. 'Do you really?'

'How long has it been?' The words were little more than a whisper. 'Since the fire?'

He felt his hands clench and forced himself to relax them. 'Twenty-three months.'

'And in all that time you haven't gone out in public?'

She made him sound like some sort of pathetic hermit, which infuriated him all the more. 'I go to work, I travel as needed, I am perfectly content as I am. Don't try to *rehabilitate* me, Milly. That's the last thing I need, trust me.' Because it wouldn't happen, no matter how hard she tried, and in the meantime she'd ruin what was between them, between her pity and his pride.

'And what about what I need?' she countered. 'A husband who can accompany me to public events, be by my side? You can't live this way for ever, Alex—'

'I can live how I choose.'

'What about if—when—we have a child?' Milly cried, her voice wavering. 'Will you still hide away then? Will you never take him or her out? Never show up for his concert or sports matches—?'

'I'm not *hiding away*.'

'That's exactly what you're doing,' she shot back.

He glared at her, fury coursing through him. He took several steadying breaths, determined to remain calm. 'You don't understand.'

'Then help me to understand,' she implored. 'Tell me what's really going on, beneath this over-the-top aversion to being seen in public.'

Yet he knew he could never do that. Tell her about the fire, about how it was his fault? Reveal to her the man he truly was, the man he was afraid he always would be? It would end everything, but perhaps that was what they needed. These last few weeks had been nothing more than a mirage anyway. The realisation was painful but necessary.

'Is this just about how people see you in public, Alex?' Milly asked quietly. 'Or is it something more?'

He stared at her for a long moment, his jaw clenched. 'I don't like to be reminded,' he finally said, the words dredged up from deep inside him.

'Of what? The accident?'

'Yes. And…' He paused, unwilling to say more, yet knowing Milly would not let it go. 'I hate people looking at me with pity. It's even worse than disgust.'

'Have you given anyone a chance?' Milly asked softly. 'Perhaps they wouldn't.'

'Don't be naïve, Milly.'

'I'm not saying everyone would be understanding or accepting. I know the world doesn't work that way, Alex. But I didn't see you the way you thought I did. I still don't, and I never will. What if you gave others the chance? What if you freed yourself from this prison of your own making?'

'It's not that simple—'

'It *is* simple, but that doesn't mean it's easy. I know that.' She gazed at him steadily, her heart in her eyes. *Her heart.* 'I know I'm asking for a great deal. I do realise that, and I *will* understand if you refuse me. But for my sake, for Anna's sake, for the family we might have one day together…will you try this once? If it all goes terribly wrong, I won't ask again.' She gave him a small, wry smile. 'At least not for a long time.'

Improbably, his mouth twitched in the smallest of smiles. 'At least you're honest.'

'I try to be. But will you do this one thing for me, Alex? Come to Rome? Go to the gala? I want to be there with you, and Anna wants it, as well. She reminded you of your sister, you said…' She trailed off uncertainly, and he knew he hadn't hid the flash of anguish he felt at the mention of his sister.

To bring Daphne into it…but Milly didn't even know what she was saying. What memories she was dredging up like old, painful ghosts, haunting him. Always haunting him.

'Please,' Milly whispered.

And even though everything in him resisted, even though he knew it would be hard and no doubt humiliating, he did the one thing he'd never expected to do. He said yes.

CHAPTER THIRTEEN

OUTSIDE THE PENTHOUSE suite stars twinkled in a darkening sky as the lights of Rome glittered below. They'd arrived in the Eternal City this morning, and the charity gala was in less than an hour.

After lunch together in their luxurious suite, Alex had insisted on Milly pampering herself at the hotel's beauty spa, as well as arranging for a stylist to come in with several incredible evening gowns for her to choose from. She'd selected a column-style gown of burgundy lace, with heels dyed to match, and had her hair swept back into a loose chignon, a few wisps framing her expertly made-up face.

Looking in the mirror, Milly hardly recognised herself, and excitement along with nerves fizzed in her stomach. She was going out for the evening...*with her husband.*

Milly had been both humbled and gratified by Alex's willingness to do this for her. They hadn't spoken again of the evening or what to expect, and now, with it looming closer, she couldn't help but worry. What if it all went horribly wrong? What if people stared and whispered, or made Alex retreat even further into himself?

She wanted to believe it wouldn't happen that way; she desperately hoped this evening could be the beginning of a new life for them both.

A new life... The words caused a fluttering of panic inside her. They had now been married for nearly two months and the pregnancy test had remained in the bottom of Milly's bag, tucked away out of sight. With each passing day, she was realising she had no need to take it; her body told its own story.

Her breasts felt fuller, and she still hadn't got her period. Even more tellingly, in the last few days she'd started feeling nauseous in the mornings. She might have been innocent but she knew enough to recognise the signs. She was almost certainly pregnant.

But if you don't take the test, you can't say for sure.

She wasn't ready to tell Alex that she was having his child. She wasn't ready for things to change between them, as she knew they would, and the fear that lodged behind her breastbone like a cold, hard stone was that once he found out she was expecting, he would send her back to Naxos and be done with her…just as he'd said he would before they'd married. One child was all he needed. He'd promised he wouldn't touch her after that.

Milly knew things had changed since they'd made that businesslike agreement…*but how much*? Despite the passion and intimacy they enjoyed in bed, in many ways Alex still felt like a stranger, cloaking himself with an emotional remoteness she was starting to hate… because he was a stranger she was falling in love with.

She certainly hadn't meant to. She'd been determined to guard her heart, had convinced herself after all the bad examples and experiences she had that she wasn't interested in love. But now Milly knew that for the fantasy it had always been. She wasn't just interested in love…she was desperate for it. Why else would she have fallen so easily for the far too glib lies of Philippe?

Because after a lifetime of living on the sidelines, being nothing more than an inconvenience to the people who were meant to love and cherish her, she longed for the kind of love that she'd read about in fairy tales, the kind of consuming, overwhelming, passionate and tender love that she wanted to believe could exist between a man and a woman.

Perhaps she'd never seen it in real life and hadn't experienced it herself—yet—but she still believed it existed. She still hoped for it.

And she couldn't risk telling Alex that she was pregnant and having it all change. Having him shut down and push her away, out of self-protection or convenience or fear. Just a few more weeks…a little more time for their relationship to grow and flourish, for Alex to realise he needed her.

Do you really think he's going to fall in love with you?

Milly turned from the view of Rome to gaze at her reflection in a gilt mirror. No matter the hairstyle, the make-up or the gown, she was still a plain little mouse. She always would be. If her own parents hadn't been able to love her, how could a man as handsome, complex, and kind as Alex? Because he *was* kind. He hid it well, but she'd seen it time and time again, the thoughtful touches, the surprising sensitivity, the tenderness. He was a good man, a wonderful, man…but how could he love her?

'Milly.' The way he spoke her name, like a caress, made a shudder of longing run through her. She would never get tired of him saying it, of him touching her, of anything about their life together. But would he? She didn't trust her own powers of persuasion. She still felt incredulous that he could desire her physically, never mind feel something deeper and more important. It was all so fragile, and she wasn't brave enough to risk it yet, even though she knew she should.

'I have something for you.' She half turned, catching her breath at the sight of him in a tuxedo, looking devastatingly as handsome as always. His dark hair was brushed back from his face, his eyes electric blue, his skin like bronze. The scars made absolutely no difference to her; he was the most handsome man she'd ever met, and he made her heart beat double-time by just looking at him.

'Turn back around,' he instructed and she did so, letting out a soft gasp as he clasped a diamond and sapphire necklace around her neck, the heavy stones cool against her skin. 'There are earrings to match.'

'Alex, it's amazing...' In the mirror the necklace, made of several large sapphire-encrusted diamonds, glittered and winked. It was the most extravagant and beautiful piece of jewellery she'd ever seen. She caught his gaze and managed a trembling smile. 'I don't know what to say...'

'They belonged to my mother,' he told her as he fastened the earrings in her ears, the gentle touch of his fingers making her shiver. 'My stepfather gave them to her on their tenth anniversary.'

The fact that they were an heirloom, part of his history, made them even more special. 'I don't even know anything about your mother,' she remarked as she touched the diamonds, watched them sparkle. 'Is she...was she...?'

'She died ten years ago. Cancer.' His tone was matter-of-fact, but his eyes were bleak, and empathy twisted inside her. 'It was better that way. Better she didn't see...'

He trailed off, his expression closing, and Milly reached up to clasp his hand resting on her shoulder. He might not want to say anything more, but she could give him that much, at least. They remained that way for a few precious seconds, with no need for words.

Then Alex stepped away. He was always the first one to do so, Milly acknowledged with a pang. Always the first to close down a conversation, to turn away, to keep it about sex. She tried not to mind, but it hurt. Every single time, it hurt. 'The limo is waiting.'

Milly reached for the matching burgundy silk wrap to cover her shoulders. Now that it was autumn, the nights were becoming chilly.

As she slid into the limo, her nerves started up again, along with the excitement. What would this evening hold? What did it promise? Maybe, just maybe, it really could be the beginning of something wonderful.

She slid a glance at Alex; he looked preoccupied, a bit stoical. She knew how hard this was for him, and she wanted to say something to encourage him, but she feared anything she said would just be a painful reminder of the challenges that lay ahead.

'Anna is so looking forward to this,' she said instead. They hadn't been able to see Anna before the gala, because of her rehearsals. 'It really is a huge honour for someone in her year to be chosen.'

'I look forward to hearing her play.'

He looked so tense that Milly ached to do something to help him relax. The limo pulled up in front of the private villa where the event was being held, an impressive eighteenth-century home just off the Piazza di Trevi. A throng of people was ascending the steps, and Milly's insides twisted with anxiety as she saw a handful of paparazzi on hand to photograph the event, something she hadn't expected. Photographs were the last thing Alex would want, and she saw his mouth tighten as he caught sight of them.

'I didn't realise...' she began, an apology, and he shook his head.

'Shall we?' His voice was toneless yet resolute. A valet opened the door of their limousine and Milly slid out, blinking as the cameras began to snap, as the paparazzi called to her in rapid-fire Italian.

'Is that Alexandro Santos?'

'Why hasn't he been seen in public in months?'

She hadn't anticipated this level of interest

and speculation. Alex would hate it. She ignored the questions as Alex got out of the car, and it was as if everyone around them drew in a collective breath. A hushed silence fell, and then the cameras began to click and snap as the questions increased in volume and urgency.

'What happened, Alex? Tell us your story.'
'Is this why you haven't been seen in public?'
'Who is accompanying you?'

Milly struggled to hold her head high, keep the smile on her face. She would not let these wretched photographers capture anything other than the pride and love she felt for her husband.

She reached for his hand, twining her fingers with his as she gave his fingers a squeeze. To her relief and joy, he squeezed back as they made their way into the villa.

This was a living hell as well as a surprising, unexpected heaven. Alex had anticipated some paparazzi to skulk around the villa, even though he knew Milly hadn't. No society event in Rome would occur without some jaded journo or other covering it. He'd known people would be shocked; he'd kept his secret well, along with his loyal staff.

He'd also known it was time to reveal it. Over the last few days he'd come to realise Milly had been right when she'd said he couldn't stay hidden away for ever, and the most surprising thing was, as painful as this felt, he didn't even *want* to hide any more.

He was married, and hoped to have a child. He couldn't live the way he had been, hiding not just from staring crowds but from life itself. This was the first important and challenging step, and he had Milly to thank for it.

No one spoke to them as they entered the villa, although Alex recognised many of the other guests. No one knew what to say. He'd kept a low profile, and so of course there had been rumours. Nervous breakdown, rehab, a top-secret deal, a consuming love affair. He'd always been a private man, and so the rumours had faded after a while as people assumed he was just keeping to himself. Now they would know the truth.

And the truth will set you free.

That, he acknowledged grimly, would be asking for too much. Still, he was here, and

Milly was by his side, looking magnificent and fiercely proud, as if she would take on anyone who dared to say something amiss. At the sight of her something unfurled in Alex, something far more tender and important than the overwhelming physical chemistry they shared. Something he craved, even as he reminded himself to keep his distance. Keep both of them safe.

Yet he could hardly keep his distance now, as they debuted in society as a married couple. Now was the time for solidarity, for togetherness, or at least its illusion.

'Alex…' A hand clapped on his shoulder, and he turned to see an old business acquaintance, Lukas Petrakis, smiling at him with a mixture of warmth and sympathy. 'I heard rumours of an accident, but they were so vague…' he said in a low voice, his gaze flicking to the left side of his face.

'Fire.' Alex kept it succinct, and Lukas nodded with a grimace.

'I'm so sorry…'

'No matter.'

'And this…?' He turned to Milly.

'This is Milly.' Alex paused. 'My wife.'

Lukas' eyebrows rose briefly but otherwise his expression remained friendly and pleasant. 'I'm so pleased to meet you. I didn't realise Alex had married.'

'Only recently,' Milly answered with a smile. 'We're newly-weds.'

'You've kept a lot quiet,' Lukas remarked, 'but then you always played your cards close to your chest.'

'Indeed.' Alex inclined his head, and they continued to move through the crowd.

It wasn't, he came to realise as the evening progressed, as agonising as he'd expected. In fact, it was more than tolerable. Yes, some people looked at him with pity, others with horrified fascination, but for the most part people were kind, sympathetic, friendly.

With Milly by his side he felt stronger, able to face anything, even as he acknowledged that some part of him had always known it wouldn't be so bad. It had been his pride along with his shame that had kept him hidden, unwilling to face people's pity as well as the reality of his own guilt every time another stranger caught sight of his scars.

It seemed his pride had now been dealt with, but as for his shame...

'Anna's playing now!' Milly whispered excitedly, and Alex retrained his focus on the small stage set up at one end of the private ballroom. As a hush fell over the crowd, Anna entered, looking young and lovely in a black velvet evening gown. She searched the crowd for a moment, her face lighting up as she caught sight of Alex and Milly. And then she began to play.

The hauntingly sad and beautiful notes of *Chaconne* by Tomaso Vitali soared through the space and wrapped around Alex's heart, each stroke of the bow on the violin seeming to reach right inside him. His fingers tightened on Milly's as he let the music breathe through him, awakening longings and hopes he could no longer keep buried, at least not in this moment.

He wanted more for his life than the cold, lonely existence he'd been trudging through day by day for the last two years, and even for his whole life. Always keeping himself apart, first from safety from his father's fists, and then from his own shame and guilt.

And he still felt the shame and guilt over

failing Daphne, but he felt something else too. *Hope.* Fragile, faint, but there. Definitely there. He glanced at Milly, and saw tears sparkling in her eyes, and with a thrill of longing he wondered if she was as affected as he was. *Felt* the way he did…

It was all so much…the music, the evening, *Milly.* His life had broken open along with his heart, and he couldn't control either any more. He didn't even want to. He clung to Milly's hand, or perhaps she clung to his. Either way they remained together, joined by their hands, the music, everything. Tonight he would tell her how he felt…

Then the piece ended, and the room was completely silent for a few taut seconds before the applause broke out, and Anna beamed.

Milly slid her hand from his as she began to clap. 'I'm so proud of her,' she murmured. 'So proud. I never thought to have a moment like this…sorry, I'm turning into an emotional wreck, aren't I?' She smiled wryly as she dashed the tears from her cheeks, and Alex came back to reality with an almighty crash.

Milly had been emotional because of *Anna,* not him. How could he have dreamed otherwise even for a moment? She didn't feel what he did, not even a little bit, and he felt biting disappointment along with an awful relief that he hadn't got to the point of declaring, and embarrassing, himself. 'Shall we go say congratulations?' he enquired, and Milly nodded.

As soon as Anna saw them, she pushed her way through the crowds, throwing her arms around Milly and then, to Alex's surprise, around him.

'I'm so glad you came!'

'Anna, you were amazing.'

'Oh, no, I flubbed a note in the second movement—'

'Truly you were,' Alex said. 'I was very touched by the music.' That was all it had been—an emotional reaction to such a sad and evocative piece.

'Yes.' Anna studied him with bright eyes, and then glanced at Milly. 'You seem happy,' she said, sounding both satisfied and hopeful.

'We're happy to be here, and to see you,' Milly said quickly. 'Of course we are.'

'Yes, we are,' Alex added swiftly. Yet another reminder. Milly seemed intent on showing him that they were there for Anna, and

Anna only. 'We must take you out for some celebratory cake and champagne.'

Anna's cheeks pinked. 'I'd love that!'

'Then it's decided.'

They celebrated in the private dining room of a nearby exclusive restaurant, with Alex ordering tiramisu and a bottle of the best champagne.

'No champagne for me,' Milly said with a little smile. 'I've had enough to drink already. But Anna can have a sip.'

Alex frowned, because as far as he recalled Milly had stuck to sparkling water at the gala, but perhaps she was remembering the last time they'd had champagne—when she'd been sick on their wedding night. A reminder he hardly wanted now. In any case, he didn't press the point, but poured Anna a small glass.

'To Anna and her stunning performance,' he said, and everyone raised their glasses. It was, Alex reflected broodingly, a reminder to him as well as a toast. Tonight had been about Anna...*only* Anna.

Both he and Milly were quiet on the way back to the hotel, having dropped Anna off at her school's boarding house. Neither of them spoke as they entered their suite, and then Milly put a hand on Alex's shoulder. He stilled.

'Alex.' She spoke his name softly.

'What is it?' His voice came out harshly; he felt too raw, after all the emotions of the evening, the impossible-to-ignore realisation that he felt something for Milly. How much, he couldn't bear to think about. Whatever it was, he could quash it down. He would have to.

'Thank you,' Milly said softly. 'Thank you for going out with me tonight. Thank you for standing by my side.' She gazed at him trustingly, her eyes wide and guileless, her expression full of sincerity and empathy.

'I should say the same,' Alex said gruffly. 'You had the harder role, undoubtedly.'

'I did not,' Milly asserted.

'Being seen with me—'

'Alex.' She pressed her finger against his lips, a whisper of skin. 'Don't say such a thing. Don't even think it. You were the handsomest man there tonight, as far as I was concerned.'

'Milly…' It came out as a warning. He did not want her pity, the useless stroking of his ego for sympathy's sake. Not now, when he'd been on the verge of feeling so much more for her.

'I mean it...' She took a step closer to him, so her hips brushed his and need, as ever, flared inside him, white-hot. 'What will it take for you to believe me?' She searched his face, looking for an answer he couldn't give because the truth was he didn't know. Then she lifted her hand and traced the deep ridges of his scars with her fingers. Alex sucked in a hard gasp, the damaged skin oversensitive, her touch achingly tender. In all the times they'd made love, she'd never touched his scars before. It felt as if she were touching his soul.

'These scars are part of who you are,' she said softly. 'They tell the story of you, and I only know part of it, but I know this: I know they show you are a survivor, and that you are strong.'

'You don't know...'

'Tell me, Alex.' She cupped his scarred cheek with her hand, and he closed his eyes, both savouring and reviling her touch. 'Tell me about the fire.'

He didn't speak for a long moment. *He couldn't.* Yet he felt the memories rising like a tide within him, and he knew he would speak. He would tell her about that terrible night. And maybe it would make her walk away from him, or at least stop trying so much, making him care whether she wanted him to or not. Perhaps telling her was the answer, the way to keep them both safe—and separate.

'It was at my house,' he finally said, the words seeming to come from far away. 'Here in Athens. I had a villa in Kolonaki.' Milly simply waited, her hand still on his cheek, touching him so tenderly. 'My sister, Daphne,' he said, knowing it was all disjointed, fragments of memory lodged in his throat—in his heart—like broken shards of glass. 'And...and her son, Talos.'

Milly's breath came out in a soft gasp of sorrow. 'Oh, Alex...'

'They both died.' He shook his head. 'I should have been able to save them.'

'How?'

Could he really tell her all of it? The terrible truth? Yes. He had to. For both of their sakes.

He took a ragged breath and opened his eyes. 'Let me start at the beginning,' he said.

CHAPTER FOURTEEN

MILLY WATCHED AS Alex walked away from her, loosening his bow tie and shedding his jacket and cummerbund. Even now, *especially* now, he looked devastatingly attractive—his body one of leashed power and innate authority, his face drawn in stark lines of remembered pain. She wanted to put her arms around him. *She wanted to tell him she loved him.*

But she didn't dare, and she knew now was not the time anyway. Now was the time for Alex's story, at last. And perhaps it would draw them closer together. She prayed it would.

'The beginning,' Alex stated flatly, 'is that my father was a terrible man. Abusive to my mother as well as to my sister Daphne and me.' Milly opened her mouth to express her horror and sorrow, but Alex cut across her before she could frame a word. 'He was clever about it, so no one knew outside the family. He always made it feel as if it were our fault—we'd done something to provoke him.' A pause as Alex stared out of the window, lost in memory. 'He would fly into terrible rages.'

'I'm sorry...'

'On the outside, we looked like the perfect family. My father was successful, my mother beautiful, Daphne and I were model children. We were too scared to be anything else. As a family we were private, because we had to be. We didn't make friends, we kept everyone as an acquaintance. It was easier that way.'

Which explained so much about Alex's need for privacy and distance now, Milly thought with an ache. He shoved his hands in his trouser pockets as he stared out at the night.

'But then my father went too far. He broke my mother's arm, and that was something she couldn't hide.' Another pause, and Milly wished he'd turn and look at her. 'I confronted him. I was fifteen by then, practically a man. And I beat him within an inch of his life. Broken nose, broken jaw, broken wrist. Internal bleeding. He was in the hospital for weeks, thanks to my fists.'

Milly couldn't keep from gasping at the awful image. She suspected he'd meant to shock her, and he had. But she still wanted to hear the rest of it.

'What happened then?' she asked softly.

'He pressed charges. My father thought he was above the law, but he wanted to make sure I wasn't.' Alex let out a rush of breath as he shrugged. 'I ended up spending a few months in juvenile detention. Not the high point of my life. But by the time I came out, my father was long gone—he'd taken a corporate job in the Middle East. And my mother was married to my stepfather, Christos.'

Milly waited, knowing there had to be more. Much more. After a long moment, Alex resumed his story. 'I was angry and impossible, but Christos took me under his wing. Treated me like his own. And I learned self-control.' He paused. 'Christos was tough on me, but in a good way. But we all had scars from my father's treatment, and that showed itself in different ways.' He paused, and Milly waited, her heart in her mouth. How much more could there be to this awful story? And yet she knew there was worse to come. He hadn't even spoken about his sister yet, not really.

'Daphne married an abusive man when she

was just twenty,' Alex resumed. 'Nikolaos Aganos. We didn't realise what was going on at first. She hid it well, but we'd all become experts at hiding. And perhaps we didn't want to realise. Perhaps we closed our eyes, because we were experts at that too. But then it got worse—it always does. And two years ago, she finally left him, running to me, bringing her four-year-old son Talos with her.' He fell silent, his expression bleak, his body taut. 'I'll never forget how she looked, coming to my door. A black eye. Bruises...bruises on her *throat*.' His voice caught, and Milly reached out a hand, desperate to comfort him even as a sense of dread seeped into her stomach. She knew Daphne was dead, and that there had been a fire...

'Oh, Alex...'

'And Talos was so terrified, he had become mute. He wouldn't say a word, just clung to her and hid his face.'

'That must have been so terrible,' Milly said quietly. Any words felt utterly inadequate. 'I'm so, so sorry.'

'You know what my reaction was?' Alex asked in that flat tone she had come to hate, except now she knew how much pain that tone-less delivery could hide. 'Anger. Just like be-fore, with my father, I felt rage—a consuming, overwhelming fury, one I could not control. And I let that guide me. I let it *drive* me. I never learn, do I?'

Milly stared at him uncertainly. 'What… what do you mean?'

'I left them there, Daphne and Talos. I left them alone in my house even though I knew they were hurting and terrified. And I went in search of Aganos. I think if I'd found him, I might have killed him.' He gave her a cold smile, the coldest she'd ever seen. 'In fact, I'm quite sure I would have.'

Milly's heart lurched as that persistent dread swirled inside her, the most corrosive of acids. 'But you didn't find him…'

'No, because while I was out in the city bay-ing for his blood, he'd gone to my house…and set fire to it.'

Milly's hand covered her mouth. 'No…'

'Yes. Daphne and Talos were sleeping. The doors were locked. When I came back, the whole place was in flames.'

So why was he the one with the scars? Milly

studied him, the clenched fists, the heaving chest, the eyes full of pain. 'You went in,' she said softly. 'Didn't you? To rescue them?'

'I didn't do much good, did I? I found them, curled up together, unconscious from the smoke. I carried them both outside, and a burning beam fell across my face as I came out of the door. But none of it mattered. They both died from smoke inhalation within the hour.'

'Oh, Alex...'

'If I'd been there—'

'But how could you have known?' Milly burst out. Realisation crashed through her, at what Alex had endured, what he had blamed himself for, for so many years. 'That fire was *not* your fault.'

'I might not have lit the match,' Alex returned staunchly, 'but I'm still to blame. I chose anger over empathy. I chose to seek personal revenge rather than to be there for my sister and her son, and as a result they both died.'

'They might have died anyway,' Milly argued, and Alex let out a harsh laugh.

'You don't really believe that.'

'You might have died as well—'

'No. The only reason Aganos came to my house was because he knew I wasn't there. He said as much in court, when he was on trial. He'd been watching the house, watching me.'

'Even so,' Milly began shakily, but then stopped. She knew whatever she said right now was crucial; she felt their relationship might turn on the words that came out of her mouth, and that thought was terrifying, because the truth was she had no idea what to say, or even what to feel.

Perhaps Alex was right, and his sister and her son *wouldn't* have died if he'd been there. Perhaps he'd let anger get the better of him more than once, but it had been a righteous anger, an anger fuelled by love and pain and the desire for justice. 'You can't torture yourself over this, Alex,' she said finally. 'Don't live your life in the past...'

'My sister and her son are *dead.*' The words came out savagely as he turned to face her. 'Because of me. And you say I should let it go? Give myself a break? Do you really think that, Milly? Or are you finally realising that I'm not the man you thought I was, have been *hoping* I was? Because that's what's been going on, isn't it?' His mouth twisted in a sneer, his scars pulling tight, his face a mask of derision. You've been starting to care for me, haven't you, no matter what you've told yourself? You've been painting rainbows in your head and now you know that you shouldn't have.' Milly blinked, his words like hammer blows to her heart, shattering it like the fragile thing she knew it had always been.

'You can't say I didn't warn you,' he continued. 'All I wanted out of this marriage was an heir, but perhaps it's better that I don't reproduce.' He lifted his chin, his eyes glittering fiercely. 'I'm not the man you've been wishing I was, Milly. Well, at least now you know. Before it's too late.'

'Too late for what?' Milly asked, her voice and body trembling. He was pushing her away on purpose, she knew it, and it hurt more than she thought possible. Her illusions were shattered…not by what Alex had admitted to, but *why* he was admitting it. Because he didn't want her to care for him. 'Do you want me to walk away from you?' she asked, her voice wobbling on the words. 'Is that what this is about, Alex?'

He shrugged a shoulder, coldly indifferent to her plea. 'You can do what you like.'

Milly swallowed hard, trying not to feel hurt. He *wanted* to hurt her, she knew that much, and that was painful enough, never mind the words he said. She was tempted to do just what he said—walk away. Save herself from any further pain. Except she knew she couldn't make that choice. Wouldn't. And yet she was so very afraid that what had been hoped to be a beginning was going to be an awful end.

'I can't walk away from you, Alex,' she said, one hand pressed to her still-flat stomach. 'Whether I want to or not.'

His mouth twisted. 'Bound by our vows?' he stated sardonically. 'How quaint, Milly—'

'No,' Milly said, and now she really was shaking, both inside and out. How had it descended to this, so quickly? She pressed her hand flat against her belly, imagining the flutter of life she knew was inside her. 'I can't, because I'm pregnant.'

Alex stared at her for a full minute, the words taking that long to penetrate his dazed mind.

He took in her terrified expression, her trembling hand on her belly.

'Pregnant,' he repeated tonelessly. 'You're sure?'

'Yes. Very.'

He continued to study her, noticing how her lips trembled along with her hand; her gaze slid away from his. She couldn't even look him in the eye. 'How far along are you?' he asked, suspicion creeping down his spine with cold fingers. 'How long have you known?'

'A...a little while.' She still wouldn't look at him.

'Milly.' His eyes narrowed as he took in other details of her appearance he hadn't realised until now: her fuller face and breasts, the slight roundness of her belly. 'How long?' he demanded harshly.

'A...a few weeks. I think we conceived on our wedding night.' She spoke softly and Alex swung around, stalking to the window as he fought a sweeping sense of betrayal—and hurt. That had been nearly two *months* ago. Why had she kept it from him? Why had she *lied*?

'Were you ever going to tell me?' he asked,

his voice low and furious. 'Or were you just going to hope for the best?'

'What is that supposed to mean?' Milly sounded near tears. 'Alex, I was going to tell you. Of course I was. It's just... I was scared.'

He swung back around. *'Scared?'*

'Yes. Scared.' She nibbled her lip, reminding him of her fear on their wedding night. The fear, it seemed, she'd always had of him, and now he'd given her even greater reason to be afraid. How could he have ever thought this would have worked? That a man like him, scarred inside and out, could love someone— and more importantly, more laughably, be loved himself?

'We can still divorce,' he heard himself saying.

'What?' Milly's eyes rounded, her jaw dropping. 'You don't mean that.'

He didn't know what he meant. He felt dazed, overwhelmed by the emotions that had spiralled through him in the course of a single evening. Realising he cared for Milly, telling her the truth, realising she didn't care about him. And now a baby. A child, the very thing he'd wanted all along...

'I don't know,' he admitted rawly. 'But at this moment it seems sensible.' He breathed out slowly, remembering what he'd told her back when they'd been ironing out all the details, how he wouldn't touch her once she was pregnant. No matter how amazing their chemistry had been, it was clear a real relationship was not possible. He was a fool to think, even for a moment, that it could have been.

'In any case,' he told her, 'now that you are carrying my child there is no reason for you to stay in Athens. You can return to Naxos tomorrow.'

Milly stared at him for a long moment, her expression impossible to read. 'Is that what you want?' she asked finally, and Alex made himself nod. It was better this way. It had to be.

'Yes,' he said. 'It is.' He paused, searching her face, trying to see if there was any affection or hope there, but she wasn't giving anything away, her face closed up, her eyes shadowed. 'I assume it is what you want, as well. You said Naxos was your home.'

Her gaze slid away from his. 'Yes...'

'So there is no difficulty.' He didn't quite make it a question, but he waited, willing her to say something. *Anything.* One word from her, he thought, and he'd take it all back. He'd demand or even beg that she stay.

But he'd put himself out there too much already tonight. He'd told her everything; he'd made himself more vulnerable than he could bear, and he didn't think he had it in him to do it again, not without a word, something from her to give him hope. Help him to believe.

And so he waited for a full heart-stopping minute, and she didn't say anything. Not one word. She just nodded slowly, and, filled with equal parts anger and pain, Alex walked out of the room.

Milly slept in the second bedroom that night; Alex heard the click of the door, and then, to his further grief and pain, the turn of the lock. Did she think he was going to invade her bedroom, demand his rights?

It took him hours to fall into an uneasy doze, and in the morning, when Alex woke, gritty-eyed after a restless night, he found that she had already gone.

'She called a taxi,' the concierge informed him apologetically when Alex confronted the man downstairs. 'Quite early…she said she was catching a morning flight back to Athens.'

'Of course.' He turned away, not willing to show a stranger how those words felled him. Clearly Milly couldn't wait to leave him. He'd expected to have her accompany him back to Athens, and then take his yacht to Naxos. But, no. She'd gone her own way, without even saying goodbye. She'd wanted quit of him as soon as she could.

It was better this way.

The words felt meaningless to him now, because it didn't feel better at all. He felt hurt and angry, filled with a grief that was deeper than he'd even imagined it could be. Yet could he really blame Milly for taking the out he'd offered?

No, he couldn't. Alex took a deep breath as he cloaked himself in a cold, icy calm. He wouldn't be angry, not this time, and he wouldn't be hurt. Neither would he care.

Yet Milly's absence ate at him all the way back to Athens, and then for the next two weeks as he heard nothing from her, and refused to reach out himself, out of both pride and hurt. He did satisfy himself that she'd got back to Naxos safely, having spoken to Yiannis, but with Milly he did not share a single word.

It was better this way.

Maybe if he kept repeating it to himself, he'd believe it one day. Believe that he could live alone and be, if not happy, then at least satisfied. But he felt neither, and every day that passed was a solitary torture.

Several times a day Alex found himself picking up the phone, starting to dial. He'd just call to see if she was all right. To check on her pregnancy. But every time he started to press her number, he stopped. He would not do it. He couldn't.

And then, three weeks after that awful night in Rome, both the beginning and end of everything, Yiannis called, his voice sounding far too grim.

'Alex,' he said. 'It's Milly.'

CHAPTER FIFTEEN

IT ALL HAPPENED SO QUICKLY. One minute Milly was walking along the dusty road to Halki, trying to enjoy the crisp autumn day and not feel the swamping of misery that had accompanied her most days since leaving Alex in Rome, and the next she was sprawled belly-down on the road, grit embedded in her hands and knees and chin, everything stinging and smarting.

Too dazed to realise what had happened, Milly simply lay there for a moment, shocked by how quickly she had fallen. Painfully she got to her hands and knees, one hand cupping her belly protectively; at fourteen weeks, she had a small, neat bump. Then she felt a trickle of hot wetness between her thighs, and everything in her clanged with panic.

Somehow she managed to get to her feet; her body ached all over and her hands, knees, and face were smeared with blood and pebbled with grit. But worse, far worse, was the fear that she was bleeding. That she might be losing this baby.

The next hour was a blur; she stumbled back to the villa, terror clutching at her as she felt a band of pain start in her lower back and radiate out. Contractions. She was having contractions, and she was so early in her pregnancy still.

'Please, no,' she gasped, and then she rang Yiannis. He was there in minutes, bundling her in his truck and taking her to the hospital in Naxos' main town.

'I must call Kyrie Santos,' Yiannis told her as she sat in a plastic chair in the hospital's crowded waiting room. Although Milly hadn't spoken of it, she knew Yiannis suspected there had been an acrimonious separation between her and Alex. 'He will want to know.'

Would he? Three weeks and there had not been one word. *Not one word.*

Milly had talked herself round and round in circles, first cursing herself for not being brave enough to tell Alex she'd fallen in love with him, and then trying to convince herself she'd done the right thing in leaving, when it had been so painfully obvious he was pushing her away. He didn't want what she wanted. He wasn't willing to take the risk. And in any case, this was what they'd agreed on, when they'd discussed those cold, clinical terms. This was what she'd expected all along.

But now all she could think about was her baby. Her precious baby, so tiny and fragile inside her. *Stay safe, baby, please...*

Yiannis left her to make the call, and when he returned his face was grim. 'Kyrie Santos is sending an air ambulance immediately to take you to Athens.'

'What? But—'

'The facilities here are not adequate for emergency maternity care,' Yiannis continued. 'Many women go to Athens for such care.' He squeezed her hand. 'It is going to be all right, Kyria Santos.'

But Milly feared it wouldn't be. And ridiculously, perhaps, it hurt that Alex was sending an ambulance rather than coming himself. He didn't care about her; it was only his precious heir that mattered. *Stay safe, baby...*

The short flight to the hospital in Athens was the loneliest and most terrifying experience of

Milly's life. The contractions and bleeding had continued, making her dread the worst. As the helicopter could only hold one patient, Yiannis had not been allowed to accompany her. She was completely on her own, and she felt it every second of the hour-long flight.

The sense of fearful loneliness continued when she arrived at the hospital in Athens, and after some initial checks, she was scheduled for an ultrasound to check on her baby. Although some of the consultants and technicians spoke English, it wasn't enough for Milly to understand whether they were reassuring or warning her, and her Greek wasn't up to the standard to ask the questions she desperately needed to.

As she waited for her scan, still not knowing what was going on or whether her baby was alive or dead, all she wanted was Alex. She'd been so stupid, so stubborn and foolish and afraid. She'd gone back over that night in Rome and rewritten it a thousand times in her head, but now, facing this alone, she knew exactly what she should have done.

She should have been brave. She should have told him she loved him, no matter how much he was trying to keep his distance, and that the regrets of his past made no difference to her. She should have held him in his arms and kissed his scars and promised him that their love could heal him. If she'd done all that, all the things that had been in her heart, perhaps she wouldn't be alone here now. Perhaps Alex would have admitted he felt something for her; perhaps he would have been brave enough to say what was in his heart.

But she hadn't done any of it, Milly acknowledged in the cold, sterile loneliness of an anonymous waiting room. She'd looked at Alex's furious face, heard his cold tone, and she'd taken him at his word and retreated. Every insecurity she'd ever had had begun to blare in her brain.

No one has ever loved you. No one has ever fought for you, or stood by you, or cared enough to take a risk. Why did you dare think this man would?

And so she'd stayed silent. And she'd let her heart break.

Worst of all, she feared now it was too late. Alex wasn't even coming to see if she was all right; in three weeks, he hadn't contacted her at all, not even to ask about their own child. If there had been a moment when he'd cared, or *could* have cared at least, it was gone. She hadn't risked her own heart, just as she'd told Alex three months ago. She'd said she hadn't seen the point, but unfortunately now she very much did. The trouble was, it was just too late.

'Where is my wife?' The words came out in a low growl of both menace and authority. The receptionist's eyes widened as she took in the full force of him, six feet three of powerful male on a mission.

'Your name, *kyrie*…?'

'Alexandro Santos,' Alex bit out. The nurse glanced at his scars but he barely noticed, hardly cared. 'And my wife is Milly Santos. She was brought here by air ambulance twenty minutes ago for a suspected miscarriage.' The words felt like a punch in the gut, leaving him breathless with pain. 'And I want to see her *immediately.*'

It had been just over an hour since Yiannis had rung him with the news that Milly had fallen and her pregnancy was threatened. An hour of raking himself over the coals, again and again, because it would *never* be enough.

How could he be failing someone he loved *again*? Having walked away *again*, instead of staying where he was needed, if not wanted? He never should have let Milly return to Naxos alone. He should have never stayed silent, too proud and ashamed to reach out to her. If something happened to the baby...*their child*...he would never forgive himself.

'Kyria Santos is in the ultrasound department,' the receptionist told him. 'If you go to the left—'

Alex went to the left. He strode down the hall, fists clenched, heart pumping. This time it *had* to work out. This time it couldn't end in tragedy and despair, not like before...

But he, more than anyone, knew there were no guarantees. No fairy promising a happy ending, waving her pointless wand. Life didn't work that way, and as he turned the corner he steeled himself for the worst.

'Alex.' Milly's voice sounded as if it were torn from her chest, a ragged cry that reached in and wrapped around Alex's heart.

He dropped to his knees in front of her,

wrapping his arms around her slight frame as she pressed her face against his shoulder, her body shaking with the force of her sobs.

'Milly…*agapi mou*…' My love. The words had slipped out, spoken from the heart, and he was glad. He put his hands on her shoulders, easing back so he could look into her face. 'Are you all right in yourself? You are not hurt…?' Her chin was smeared with blood, a bruise on one cheekbone. It made Alex ache.

'Just scraped.' Milly sniffed. 'But, Alex, the baby, our baby…'

A fist closed over his heart. 'You have had the scan?'

'Not yet. But I've…' She dropped her voice along with her eyes. 'I've had bleeding and contractions…oh, Alex, I'm so scared.'

He pulled her to him again, stroking her hair as he offered her words of comfort. *Agapi mou. Kardia mou.* My love. My heart. He didn't know if she understood what they meant, but he couldn't keep himself from saying them. From meaning them. Now that she was in his arms again, the life of their child in danger, he knew he meant them more than anything he'd ever said in his life.

He loved her. And he would tell her, whether she loved him or not. She deserved to know. He wanted her to know. He needed it.

'Milly Santos?'

They both tensed at the sound of her name on the nurse's lips. Alex helped her rise shakily to her feet and then he accompanied her into a darkened room for the scan.

'Please make yourself comfortable,' the nurse instructed. 'The technician will be with you shortly.'

Moments later the technician came in, a kindly-looking woman with a sympathetic smile. Alex watched, his heart caught in his throat, as Milly lifted her shirt, revealing the slight swell of her baby bump. *Their child*, right there. Tears clogged his throat and he swallowed hard. *Their child.*

'Let's see how baby is doing,' the technician murmured in Greek, and they both waited breathlessly as she squirted the cold, clear gel on Milly's stomach and then began to swipe and probe with the wand. Within seconds an image appeared on the screen, black and white and blurry. Their baby.

And it wasn't moving.

'*Alex...*' Milly's hand grabbed hold of his hand, and he held on tightly, wanting to imbue her with his strength. His hope. *Please, God. Please, not this time...*

And then, like the miracle it truly was, the tiny form on the screen flung out an arm. The technician turned up the volume on the ultrasound machine and the room was suddenly filled with a loud whooshing noise.

'Baby's heartbeat,' the technician explained. 'Sounds a bit like a galloping horse.'

'You mean...the baby is okay?' Milly asked tremulously, in halting Greek. She turned to Alex. 'Can you ask her...? I don't understand enough Greek...'

'Of course.'

He spoke swiftly to the technician, and then turned back to Milly, unable to keep the emotion from his voice, his eyes. 'The baby is all right. Perfectly healthy. They want to keep you in hospital for a few days, and then bed-rest for a while after that, because the contractions are a concern. But everything looks okay, Milly.' He broke off, finding it hard to speak. 'Our baby is going to be all right.'

They didn't talk as Milly was taken in a

wheelchair to a hospital room, the best Alex could procure. She looked exhausted, her face pale and grey with fatigue, and Alex knew she needed to sleep.

'Alex...' she began, sounding uncertain, and gently he pressed his fingers against her lips.

'Shh. You need to sleep. We can talk later, Milly.' He settled himself into a chair by the bed. 'I'm not going anywhere.'

She nodded slowly, her eyelids already fluttering, and within minutes she was asleep.

Milly woke slowly, blinking the hospital room into focus as memories rushed through her. The fall. The ambulance. *Alex.*

She turned her head, her heart leaping into her throat at the thought that he might have left, but he was there, just as he'd promised he would be. His unmarked cheek was resting on his hand, his scarred cheek turned to her, his eyelids drooping in sleep. He looked wonderful.

Alex's eyes fluttered open and then his electric-blue gaze trained on her and he straightened. 'You're awake.'

'Yes.'

He leaned forward, scanning her face. 'How do you feel?'

'Aching all over. And still so tired.' Tremulously, wanting to be brave, she reached for his hand. He took it, twining his fingers with hers. 'Alex…'

'Wait.' His voice was rough. 'Don't say anything, Milly.'

Her heart felt like a bird fluttering in her chest. 'Why not?' she whispered.

'Because I want to say something first.'

She swallowed hard. She had no idea what he was going to say, but she feared it. He looked so serious, so intent. 'All right,' she finally managed.

Alex bowed his head. Several moments passed before he looked up again, and when he did Milly saw the sheen of tears in his eyes. 'Milly, I'm sorry. So, so sorry.'

'For…what?'

'For letting you down. I never should have… there are so many things I shouldn't have done.' He drew a shuddering breath. 'I shouldn't have assumed things on our wedding night that made it such a disaster. I shouldn't have asked to have the marriage annulled. I shouldn't have pushed you away, time and time again, because…because I was a coward. An emotional coward.'

'Alex…'

'And most of all, I shouldn't have kept myself from telling you that I love you.'

Milly felt as if her heart had somersaulted in her chest. For a few seconds she couldn't make sense of the words, was afraid to trust them. 'You…'

'Love you. Yes. I think I fell in love with you right from the beginning, although I convinced myself I felt nothing. And over these last few weeks…the time we've spent together…the courage and kindness you've shown…'

'Courage!' Milly let out a trembling laugh. 'I was as much a coward as you, Alex. Why do you think I said nothing that night in Rome?'

He winced, shaking his head. 'That was my fault…'

'It was mine, as well. After so many years of feeling pushed aside and unloved, I let those fears govern my head and heart. I wanted to tell you I'd fallen in love with you, but I didn't because I was scared.' She shook her head, regret turning her voice ragged. 'It was the same reason I didn't tell you I was pregnant. I was afraid that once you found out I was, you'd send me away. Tell me you didn't need or want me any more.'

Alex grimaced. 'And that's just what I did, because I thought it was for the best...except I didn't, really. I didn't at *all*. The last three weeks have been hell for me, Milly. I've picked up the phone a dozen times a day to ring you, but I never did, because I was too proud. Too afraid.' He shook his head. 'And I left you alone while you were pregnant...if something had happened to our child...'

She reached over to take his hand between both of her own. 'Alex, you have carried the weight of the world on your shoulders for too long. You can't blame yourself for everything.'

'But if I'd been there—'

'I still would have walked into Halki on my own. Do you really think you could have stopped me? And if it hadn't been a walk into the village, it might have been on the stairs, or going down to the beach... You're not God, Alex. You can't control everything, and you can't blame yourself every time something goes wrong.'

He was silent for a long moment, staring down at their clasped hands. 'But it was my anger, my pride and my shame that kept us apart, just as before. I was too proud to admit I was wrong, and too ashamed to risk telling you how I felt.'

'But you are now,' Milly said softly. Her heart was filling up to overflowing with hope and happiness. 'And that's what matters. What we say *now*. The past is in the past, Alex…all the pain and hurt and regret. It's shaped who we are, but it doesn't have to shape our future. It can't be changed, but it can be redeemed.'

'Do you really believe that?' he asked hoarsely.

'Yes, with all my heart.'

Alex looked at her, his hand still clasped between hers, his expression utterly serious. 'Did you mean what you said, Milly? About having fallen in love with me?'

Her mouth was dry, tears brimming in her eyes, as she answered. 'With all my heart.'

'Why?'

He sounded so incredulous, she couldn't help but laugh. 'Because you're wonderful, Alexandro Santos. You're kind and thoughtful and courageous and honest. And you're quite handsome, as well.'

'Handsome—' he scoffed, but she shook her head, pressing her palm against his scarred cheek.

'Devastatingly handsome and sexy to boot. I love you, Alex. I've fallen in love with you over the last few months, and I want to spend the rest of my life loving you, if you'll let me.' It felt so good to say the words, so freeing and wonderful. Not scary after all, in the end, and definitely worth the risk.

'If I'll let you? I'll count myself blessed to do so. All I want to do is make up for lost time, Milly, and love you for the rest of my days.'

'Starting now?' Milly said softly.

Alex placed his hand on her slight bump, a look of wonder on his face. 'And lasting for ever.'

EPILOGUE

Six months later

'IT'S A GIRL!'

Alex let out an incredulous laugh as the doctor lifted the squalling, red-faced baby onto Milly's chest. Tears streamed down her cheeks as she touched the damp, dark ringlets of their infant daughter. 'She's perfect.'

'She looks like you,' Alex said as he dropped a kiss onto her forehead. It had been an intense twenty hours of labour, and Milly had been amazing throughout, as brave as he'd ever seen her be.

'Like me?' Milly scoffed as the nurse placed her daughter in her arms. 'She looks like you. Dark hair and blue eyes. Beautiful.'

'Her eye colour might change,' the nurse said with a smile.

'Either way, she's perfect,' Alex stated definitively. 'Because she's ours.'

'Yes.' Milly cooed down at her daughter. They hadn't talked too much about names, not daring to hope so much. It had been a difficult pregnancy, and Milly had gone into pre-term labour several times before the doctors had been able to stop it. She'd been on bed-rest for four months, and their daughter had finally been born at a healthy thirty-eight weeks, to both of their relief. They'd both been afraid they might never reach this moment, but they had. And while the last six months had been scary, they'd also been wonderful, for the uncertainty of their situation had brought them together, stronger and more in love than ever.

They'd learned to turn *towards* each other when they were frightened or worried, rather than away. They'd come to depend on each other utterly, and for that they were both thankful, as well as for the miracle lying in Milly's arms.

'Have you thought of a name?' Alex asked softly as he gazed down at the Madonna-like picture of his wife holding their child.

'I have,' Milly admitted, her gaze on their daughter. 'If it was all right with you, I was thinking of Daphne.'

Alex blinked rapidly, moved by her suggestion. 'If you really mean it…'

'Of course I do.' Milly looked up at him, her beautiful face suffused with love and tenderness. 'Would you like to hold her, Alex? Would you like to hold your daughter?'

Wordlessly, unable to frame the words, he nodded. Gently Milly transferred their daughter to him and Alex cradled her tiny form, amazed and humbled by the slight and yet overwhelming weight of her. His daughter. Daphne.

As Milly had told him all those months ago, the past could not be changed, but it could be redeemed. *He* could be redeemed, and the proof of it was here in his arms, by his side. His daughter. His wife. *His family.* For ever.

Turning back to Milly, Alex reached for her hand. In that moment, they needed no words, nothing but the joining of their fingers, their hearts. Together. Always. Her eyes full of love, Milly smiled at him, and with his heart overflowing, everything in him singing with joy, Alex smiled back.

* * * * *

LET'S TALK
Romance

For exclusive extracts, competitions
and special offers, find us online:

f facebook.com/millsandboon

⊙ @millsandboonuk

🐦 @millsandboon

Or get in touch on 0844 844 1351*

For all the latest titles coming soon,
visit millsandboon.co.uk/nextmonth